Tessa leaned against the wall and waited, her breath lodged in her throat, her pulse pounding.

A minute later, he was back. "All clear."

She let go of the breath she'd been holding. "How do people live like this?"

"Like what?" he asked.

She shook her head. "In fear of walking into their own home?"

"We'll catch that guy. He's got to slip up soon. Hopefully they'll locate the vehicle that he used as a battering ram and trace him through that."

"Unless he stole it," Tessa suggested.

"If he was smart, that's what he'd have done," Irish said.

He led her into the house, turned, closed and locked the door behind them. "The question is, what did you do to tick him off?"

HELD HOSTAGE AT WHISKEY GULCH

New York Times Bestselling Author

ELLE JAMES

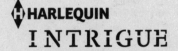

This book is dedicated to my children, whom I love dearly.
When life gets me down, they rally around me and lift me up.
I can always count on them to be there for me, and they can count on me to be there for them. I love them so very much and feel blessed that they are mine.

For you, Courtney, Adam and Megan.
With love,
Mom

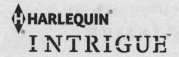

HARLEQUIN®
INTRIGUE™

Recycling programs for this product may not exist in your area.

ISBN-13: 978-1-335-48944-9

Held Hostage at Whiskey Gulch

Copyright © 2022 by Mary Jernigan

This edition published by arrangement with Harlequin Books S.A.

For questions and comments about the quality of this book, please contact us at CustomerService@Harlequin.com.

Harlequin Enterprises ULC
22 Adelaide St. West, 41st Floor
Toronto, Ontario M5H 4E3, Canada
www.Harlequin.com

Printed in U.S.A.

Elle James, a *New York Times* bestselling author, started writing when her sister challenged her to write a romance novel. She has managed a full-time job and raised three wonderful children, and she and her husband even tried ranching exotic birds (ostriches, emus and rheas). Ask her, and she'll tell you what it's like to go toe-to-toe with an angry 350-pound bird! Elle loves to hear from fans at ellejames@earthlink.net or ellejames.com.

Books by Elle James

Harlequin Intrigue

The Outriders Series

Homicide at Whiskey Gulch
Hideout at Whiskey Gulch
Held Hostage at Whiskey Gulch

Declan's Defenders

Marine Force Recon
Show of Force
Full Force
Driving Force
Tactical Force
Disruptive Force

Mission: Six

One Intrepid SEAL
Two Dauntless Hearts
Three Courageous Words
Four Relentless Days
Five Ways to Surrender
Six Minutes to Midnight

Visit the Author Profile page at Harlequin.com.

CAST OF CHARACTERS

Joseph "Irish" Monahan—Former Delta Force soldier who left active duty to make a life out of the line of fire. Working for Trace Travis at the Whiskey Gulch Ranch.

Tessa Bolton—Nurse, former cheerleader and homecoming queen. Escaped an abusive marriage and moved back to her hometown to start over.

Trace Travis—Former Delta Force who shares his inheritance with his father's bastard son and builds a security agency employing former military.

Matt Hennessey—Prior service, marine and town bad boy, now half owner of the Whiskey Gulch Ranch.

Randy Hudson—Tessa's ex-husband, former high school quarterback and homecoming king.

Nathan Harris—Former football player from Tessa's high school senior class, now driving big rigs across the country.

Wayne Payton—Former football player from Tessa's high school senior class, now installing cable and internet in Whiskey Gulch.

Connor Daniels—Former football player from Tessa's high school senior class, now a firefighter in Whiskey Gulch.

Hayden Severs—Former football player from Tessa's high school senior class, now a tow truck driver in Whiskey Gulch.

Penny Stevens—High school cheerleader in Tessa's class murdered on graduation night in Whiskey Gulch.

Dallas Jones—Former US Army Military Police, working as a deputy sheriff in Whiskey Gulch.

Chapter One

Tessa Bolton retied the shoestring on her running shoe and straightened. Though the sun had yet to rise completely, the day promised to be clear and beautiful.

She inhaled deeply, raised her hands above her head and released the air out of her lungs. After a few stretches, she was ready to follow the trail along the river's edge, her usual morning jog that got her day off to a good start.

A figure appeared in the gray light of dawn, coming toward her as she started down the path.

She tensed for a second before she realized who it was. A smile curled the corners of her lips and she raised a hand in greeting.

"Good morning," Tessa called out.

Joseph "Irish" Monahan slowed his jog to a walk as he approached. "We have to quit meeting like this," he said with a wink. "You'll start thinking I'm stalking you."

She laughed. "If anything, you'll think I'm stalking you. You're always here well before me."

"I like to run before the sun comes up. Always did in the army. That way I can beat the heat."

Droplets of sweat dripped off his forehead and his naked chest and shoulders glistened in the soft haze of morning. He always ran without a shirt, the sweat enhancing his muscular physique. The man was one-hundred-percent eye candy.

Tessa swallowed hard to force back her desire to run her fingers across his chest to test the hardness of his muscles. "You're not in the army now," she pointed out,

"No, but I work for someone else, and I like to get there early." He shrugged his broad shoulders. "You know, lots of mouths to feed."

She chuckled. "As in horses, cows and chickens?"

He nodded, a grin spreading across his face. "I rarely hear a complaint about the chow served in the mess hall."

"I would think the country life would be boring after all those years in the Special Forces." She tilted her head. "You were Delta Force, right?"

He dipped his head. "I was. Best years of my life."

Tessa's brow furrowed. "If they were the best years, why did you leave the army?"

His gaze shifted from hers to somewhere over her shoulder. "I was ready to get on with my life. When you're Delta, you tend to put the rest of your life on hold."

She frowned. "I don't understand."

His gaze returned to hers. "It's hard to have any kind of relationship outside your team when you're never home. I didn't risk getting married, only to be divorced within a year." He shrugged. "I saw too many of my buddies go through that."

"So, you gave up the military and came to Whiskey Gulch to get married?" Her lips twitched as she fought to hide her smile.

His forehead creased. "I wouldn't say that. I left the military to discover what real life is all about. And I was getting too old to hold up under the physical demands of the job."

Her gaze swept him from head to toe, finding him perfectly fit. "I doubt you had any trouble keeping up with the younger guys."

"Yeah, but it was only a matter of time before my luck ran out. A stray bullet, flipped vehicle, or shrapnel from an IED or mortar round would have put me out of commission and the army. As it was, I left on my own terms."

Tessa grabbed her ankle and pulled it up behind her, stretching her leg. "And working with the animals will keep you satisfied with life?"

His lips curved. "Among other things. The boss, Trace, has other activities in mind for us and he's bringing on other men like me to handle them."

"Really?" She dropped her ankle and reached for the other, pulling it up behind her. "What kind of activities?"

He lifted a shoulder. "Some kind of security service. We're all trained soldiers, we have skills not usually found in the civilian world. He has an idea that we can use our training to help others."

"Sounds admirable. Whiskey Gulch is a small town. Will you find enough of that kind of work here? I'd think you'd have to be in a more populated area to warrant starting a security service."

"Trace thinks if we start it, word will get out. People will find us." Irish shrugged. "In the meantime, I have animals to feed and care for. They're therapeutic."

"And after all you've been through as a Delta Force operative, you could use some downtime." Tessa smiled. "Thank you for your service."

His cheeks reddened. "I'd better get going." He frowned, his gaze going to the river trail. "You all right to run alone?"

Tessa lifted her chin. "I've done it every morning for the past few months. I'll be fine."

"Same route every day?"

She nodded. "I'm trying to improve my time."

"You should really alter your route. Never do the same one twice. Be a little more random."

She laughed. "What could happen out here? We're in the middle of nowhere."

Irish's eyes narrowed. "I make it a habit to never say what could happen. It's like tempting fate to throw something in your path. Something bad."

She planted her hands on her hips. "Are you telling me this tough Delta Force soldier is superstitious?"

He crossed his arms over his chest. "Damn right I am. Intuition saved my butt more times than I can remember."

"I don't believe in luck, fate or intuition. Knowledge is what you have to bank on."

"You're a nurse, right?"

Her brow dipped. "Yes. So?"

"Don't you base some of your work on instinct?"

She shook her head. "I don't call it instinct. I call it experience. I don't leave my patients' lives up to fate or hunches."

Irish tipped his head. "Believe what you will. I still think luck and intuition play a major part in our lives and the paths we choose or are chosen for us." He glanced toward the trail along the river's edge. "Sure you don't want me to run with you?"

Tessa shook her head. "No. You have hungry subjects to feed. I'll be fine." She turned to leave.

"Tessa?" Irish called out to her.

She glanced over her shoulder. "Yes?"

He opened his mouth, must have thought better of it, and closed it again. He gave her a crooked smile. "Nothing. Have a good run." He turned, climbed into his truck and drove away.

For a long moment, she stared after him. If she wasn't mistaken, he'd been about to…what? Ask her out? See if she wanted to get coffee? Tell her he was ready to start working toward that life after the army, and he wanted to test the waters with her?

Tessa shook her head. Sure, she found Irish attractive. If he asked her out, she probably would say yes. But that didn't mean they were headed down the path of happily-ever-after. She had too much baggage of her own to waltz down that lane.

Once bitten, twice shy?

That was Tessa to a tee. Her ex-husband had ruined her for other men. His abuse had left her little more than a shell of herself. Over the past few months, she'd worked to regain her self-esteem and rebuild her confidence. She'd be damned if she let another man drag her down again.

Not that Irish would do that.

Tessa rolled her shoulders to ease the tension that always came with memories of Randy. He'd sucker punched her with his fists and words on more than one occasion.

She'd indulged in comfort food until she was fifty pounds overweight.

Randy Hudson, being the jerk he was, had ridiculed her over her weight, along with all her other perceived faults, which had only made her sink deeper into depression.

One day, she'd looked at herself in the mirror and found a stranger looking back. That day, she'd decided enough was enough. She'd thrown out the brand-new carton of Rocky Road ice cream, put on her sneakers and gone for a walk.

Walking became running and she only ate to fuel her body, not to feed her depression.

When Randy criticized her, she stood up to him, telling him that she wasn't going to take it anymore. He either had to quit disrespecting her or she would leave.

Well, she'd ended up in Whiskey Gulch where

she'd grown up, and Randy had remained in San Antonio.

Leaving him, getting the divorce, starting over, had been the best decision of Tessa's life. She'd shed the fifty pounds plus an extra ten. Never in her life had she felt better physically and been more content with her life.

But she had to admit, she missed having someone in her life. Tessa hadn't dated since her divorce. She wasn't confident about her choice in men. When she'd met and married Randy, she'd been certain he was the perfect man for her.

Boy had she been wrong.

How could she be certain the next man she decided to date wouldn't be another Randy?

For weeks, she and Irish had bumped into each other, crossing paths at the river trail. She'd be lying to herself if she didn't admit that she found him attractive.

Randy had been good-looking as well. Good looks weren't everything. The next man in Tessa's life had to be kind-hearted and nonjudgmental. Supportive, not destructive.

So far, Irish had been nothing but a gentleman. She'd been tempted.

Shrugging off her thoughts about the former Delta Force operative, Tessa slipped her earbuds in her ears, set her music to her running playlist and took off down the river path.

Her feet hit the ground in time to the songs, the playlist motivating. She'd had the same music now for a couple of months. The familiarity with the different songs let her know where she was in her workout. When she heard the strains of "Born to Run" by Bruce Springsteen, she knew she was halfway, and it was time to turn around for the jog back.

She'd been running for twenty minutes when she passed through a wooded area with weeping willow trees hanging low overhead. With Duran Duran in her ear, she didn't hear the sound of footsteps or the rustle of leaves until a figure burst out of the willow branches, dressed in dark clothes with a black ski mask over his face, and blocked the path.

Tessa let out a sharp squeal and dodged to the left to avoid running into the man.

He moved faster, grabbing her arm with hands encased in the kind of gloves used for good grip in sports.

Tessa dug her feet into the dirt, twisted and pulled to free herself from his grasp, to no avail.

He punched her in the side of her face, yanked her around and caught her in a headlock, clamping his arm around her neck.

Her pulse raced and her vision blurred. Tessa fought for her life. When her struggles didn't free her, she stilled, trying to remember the self-defense lessons she'd taken before she'd left San Antonio. It all came back to her.

Tessa went limp in the man's arms.

He fumbled to hold her upright.

As the man bent over to steady her, Tessa bunched her legs beneath her and pushed against the earth, rising up so fast, he didn't have time to move out of her way.

Tessa's head hit the man beneath his jaw, whipping his head up and back. His arm loosened around her neck.

Tessa shoved his elbow upward and ducked beneath it, slipping behind him. Planting a foot on his backside, she kicked hard, sending him flying into the willow tree.

Before her attacker could regain his balance, Tessa ran as fast as she could to get back to where she'd parked her car by the road.

She'd only gotten halfway there when he slammed into her from behind.

Tessa hit the ground on her hands and knees, oblivious to the pain of gravel scraping against her skin. The man on her back grabbed her by her ponytail and pulled her head back.

"You'll pay for that," he said, his voice low and threatening, his breath hot against her ear.

On her belly, pinned to the ground, Tessa flailed her arms and legs. Nothing she did could shake him from her back.

He grabbed her arm, shifted to one side and attempted to roll her onto her back.

As she rolled onto her side, she cocked her arm and slammed her elbow into the man's face.

He cried out, clutched his face with both hands and rocked on his haunches.

Tessa shoved him hard, sending him flying to land flat on his back.

With only seconds to spare, she scrambled to her feet and ran, refusing to look around. She could hear the sound of his footsteps on the gravel behind her as she reached her vehicle where she'd left it what seemed like hours ago.

Her heart pounding, she pulled the key fob from the tiny pocket in her shorts, hit the unlock button, yanked open the door and flung herself inside.

With her hand shaking, she fumbled to get the key into the ignition.

Out of the corner of her eye, she saw movement. He was almost to her.

Her heart leaped into her throat as she slammed her hand down on the button that locked the doors.

The man in the ski mask grabbed her door handle and yanked hard. When it didn't open, he pounded his fists against the window.

Terrified, Tessa shoved her shift into drive.

Her attacker flung himself onto her hood and pounded the front windshield with his fists.

Tessa hit the accelerator, jerked the steering wheel right then left and spun in the gravel.

The guy on her hood slid from side to side, holding on, refusing to let go.

Tessa gunned the accelerator shooting the vehicle forward. Then she slammed on her brakes.

The man on the hood slid off onto the ground.

Tessa pushed the shift into Reverse and backed away as fast as the vehicle would go. She made it to the paved road and kept going in reverse, heading toward town. When she'd gotten far enough away from her attacker, she spun the steering wheel, shifted into Drive and raced toward Whiskey Gulch. Her cell phone would have been little use with reception spotty that far from town and the transmission tower.

Tessa didn't slow until she saw the first houses on the outskirts of town. Even then, she flew down Main Street, coming to a skidding stop in front of the sheriff's office.

The sheriff and another man were standing out front when she stumbled out of the SUV and ran up the steps.

The other man was Irish, now dressed in lightweight workout pants. He turned, a frown pressing his eyebrows together. "Tessa?"

"Help," she cried and threw herself at the unsuspecting man.

Chapter Two

Irish wrapped his arms around Tessa and held her tight. "Hey, what's wrong? What happened?"

The sheriff reached out and touched Tessa's arm. "Are you all right, Miss Bolton?"

She shook her head, burrowing her face against Irish's chest. "He grabbed me."

Irish stiffened. "Who grabbed you?"

Tessa shook her head. "I don't know. He wore a mask. He grabbed me in a chokehold. I...almost... didn't get away." Her body shook as she sobbed in Irish's arms.

He tipped her head up and stared down into her watery eyes. "Where was this? On the river trail?"

She nodded. "I've never...had this...happen," she said between gulps of air and sobs.

"Do I need to get an ambulance?"

Tessa dismissed his question. "No. I got myself here. I can get myself home."

Sheriff Barron shook his head and reached for the radio mic on his shoulder. "I'll send a unit out to the trail now."

"Please," Tessa said. "You have to catch him."

"We'll do our best," the sheriff said as he ducked back inside the office, calling out orders as he went.

"Where are you hurt?" Irish asked, staring at her face, his thumb tracing a red mark near her temple.

Tessa winced and captured his hand. "He hit me in the side of the head. Then he wrapped his arm around my neck." She raised her other hand to her throat.

"How did you get away?" he asked.

Tessa shook her head. "I went limp. When he loosened his hold, I came up fast and head-butted his chin."

Irish gave her a gentle smile. "You're smart."

"I took self-defense training in San Antonio before I moved back here." She snorted. "I almost forgot everything I'd learned."

"Apparently, you didn't." His hand squeezed hers.

Tessa's eyes rounded. "Or I wouldn't be here now."

"Thank God." Irish gently touched the top of her head. "We should have you checked out."

When he tried to set her at arm's length, she clung to him, her body trembling. "I've never been more frightened in my life," she whispered.

Irish smoothed a hand over her burnished red hair no longer contained in the ever-present, tight ponytail she'd worn earlier. "All the more reason to get you to a hospital and have them check you out for concussion."

"No," she said. "I'm okay."

Uncertain, he held her away from him. "At the

very least, you need those scrapes on your knees taken care of."

She tipped her head toward the building. "I'm sure the sheriff's got a first-aid kit."

Irish's eyes narrowed. "I'd rather have a doc take a look." When her brow furrowed, he held up his hands. "But if a first-aid kit is what you want, by all means, let's get that." He held open the door for her and guided her through with a hand at the small of her back.

The woman manning the front desk hurried around the partition wall. "Oh, Tessa, sweetie. I heard what happened to you." She moved aside and gestured toward her seat. "Here, take my seat."

"No, Ramona. I'm okay." Tessa smiled. "Besides, you're working."

"It's fine," Ramona said, pointing to her headset with the mic next to her mouth. "Bluetooth is amazing." She headed to a closet at the far side of the room. "We have a first-aid kit in here somewhere." She opened the door to find the kit secured to the other side. "We don't use it that often. But it's here for just such an occasion. What do you need?"

Irish led Tessa to Ramona's seat and urged her to sit. "We could use something to clean the wounds and bandages to cover them."

Tessa collapsed into the padded chair, shaking. She clasped her hands in front of her as if to still them.

The sheriff strode back through the office, heading for the door. He stopped in front of Tessa. "I'm on my way out to the river road to see if we can find anything to lead us to your attacker. Think you can show us where he attacked you?" He held up his hand. "If it's too traumatic, I don't expect you to go, but it would help to know exactly where it happened. We might find some evidence that could lead us to the perpetrator."

Tessa pushed to her feet, her back stiffening. "Anything I can do to help catch the guy." She shuddered. "I hate to think of him attacking another woman who might not get away."

Irish frowned. "After we take care of those scrapes." He opened an alcohol packet, knelt in front of her and looked up into her eyes. "This might sting."

"Just do it," she said, and sank back into Ramona's chair.

He swiped the pad over her skinned knee.

Tessa sucked in a sharp breath but didn't cry out.

It had to be stinging. Irish admired her even more. She refused to show weakness.

After applying a bandage to the knee, he treated the other. Then he took her hands in his. "Any scrapes here?"

She pulled them free. "Nothing I can't live with," she said. "The sooner we get out to the river road, the better chance we have of catching that guy."

"More than likely, he's long gone," the sheriff said. "But we might find some clues as to who it was. And brace yourself, I'll be asking some pointed questions. In many cases, victims know their attackers."

Irish clenched his fists. "All the more reason to wear a ski mask. We need to find the bastard."

The sheriff nodded toward Tessa and then the door. "Are you following me in your own vehicle?"

Tessa opened her mouth.

Before she could speak, Irish answered for her. "She'll ride with me." He glanced at her. "If that's okay with you?"

She gave him a shaky smile. "Thanks. I got myself here, but I'm not so sure I could drive back out to where it happened without falling apart."

He took her hand in his and squeezed gently. "Hang in there. You're not alone now."

She dipped her head. "And I'm glad. I've never felt more vulnerable. Even when…"

Irish's eyes narrowed. "Even when what?"

"Oh, nothing." Tessa squared her shoulders. "Let's do this. That man can't be allowed to run free. Since he didn't get me, he might go after some other lone female." She drew in a deep breath and led the way out the front of the building. "I couldn't live with myself if he hurt someone else."

"He's the one with the problem. You aren't responsible for his actions," Irish said, following her to the parking lot. He waved toward his pickup. "Leave your car here, for now. I'll bring you back."

"Aren't you supposed to be at work out at Whiskey Gulch Ranch?" she asked.

"Trace will understand. I'll call him as soon as we're in the pickup. This is just the kind of thing he'd want to help with."

Tessa paused at the door to his truck and looked up into his eyes, her brow creasing. "What do you mean? Trace owns a ranch. Why would he think this is something he could work?"

"Trace Travis inherited his father's ranch, yes, but he still feels the need to protect and serve." Irish grinned. "And to use the skills he acquired and mastered as a Delta Force operative in the army. He's set up a security business."

"Is that why he hired you?"

Irish nodded. "There are three of us now, counting Trace. But we have more coming on board as they separate from the service."

"It's nice that our men in uniform have a place to work outside of the military," Tessa said as she climbed into the passenger seat of Irish's truck. "I worked with veterans coming home from war, getting out of the military. The struggle to find themselves in the civilian world is real."

"No kidding." Irish slid into the driver's seat and pulled out of the parking lot, following the sheriff down the highway that led out of Whiskey Gulch. "But all that aside, I'm worried about you."

Tessa sighed. "I'm okay. He didn't get me."

"He almost did."

"My self-defense training saved me."

"This time," Irish said.

Tessa shot a frown toward Irish. "Surely, after failing to capture me, he won't try again. Will he? I mean, he didn't get me. Will he go after an easier target?"

Irish shrugged. "We can only guess about his motivation and intention. He could have chosen you as a crime of opportunity."

Tessa nodded. "That's what I was thinking."

"Or he could have targeted you specifically." Irish glanced her direction in time to see her swallow hard.

"But why?" she whispered.

"I don't know." Irish paused before asking, "Have you made an enemy out of one of your patients?"

Tessa shook her head. "My patients love me."

Irish grinned. "That, I could believe." He reached out and bussed her under her chin with his knuckles. "What's not to love?"

She snorted. "A lot. I'm sure I've pissed off someone along the way. I just can't remember who." Her brow dipped low. "Really. Not one person comes to mind."

"Because you're such a nice person. How could anyone be mad at you?" As he navigated through town, he reached out and took her hand in his. "Do me a favor and don't go running along the river without a buddy."

"I need to exercise," she said, staring down at her hand in his. "It's what helped me through a rough time."

"Yeah?" he prompted, hoping she'd open up about her rough time, but giving her the option of ignoring his prompt.

She sat silent for several seconds. "My ex-husband gave me hell when I left him."

Irish's hand tightened around hers. "How so?"

"He didn't want the divorce."

"Why did you divorce him?" Irish started to let go of her hand. "You don't have to answer. It's none of my business."

Tessa's fingers curled around his, holding tightly. "No. It's okay. I guess I'd had enough." She stared through the window, her jaw hardening. "The last time he broke my ribs, I realized he wasn't going to change. He couldn't control his anger, and I wouldn't survive the next time he lost it."

Irish swore softly, his hand on the steering wheel squeezing hard. Any man who hit a woman was not a man in Irish's books. "I'm sorry," he said softly.

"Why? You didn't hit me. I stayed in the situation too long. I should have left sooner."

"I'm sorry you had to endure it," Irish said softly. "Is that why you took self-defense classes?"

Tessa nodded. "Randy ignored the restraining order all too often. He didn't like losing. Even if he didn't love me, he didn't like the fact that I'd left *him*. He took it as if he'd lost a game." She grunted. "I just wanted to be free of fear. I moved home from San Antonio to get away from Randy."

"You think he might have come here to seek revenge?" Irish asked.

Tessa paused. "I don't know, but I don't think it was him. I mean it's been a while since I left my ex. Why would he seek revenge now? Besides, the man on the trail was a taller than my ex. And maybe stronger?" She shrugged. "It all happened so fast, I can't recall everything about him. The whole attack was such a blur."

"So, you're not exactly sure of his height and build?"

Her mouth twisted. "No. I just didn't feel like it was Randy."

"It might not hurt to check on his whereabouts," Irish stated. "Let the sheriff know."

She nodded. "I will." Tessa shivered as they pulled off the road onto the gravel parking area beside the river where Irish usually found Tessa's vehicle parked after his run.

Irish turned to her. "You don't have to do this, you know."

She drew in a deep breath and let it go. Then, squaring her shoulders, she gave a brief nod. "I need to show him where it went down. If they can find anything that would lead to catching my attacker, it would be worth the effort."

"True." The trail along the river was bordered by brush, tall grass and trees. She didn't expect it to be easy to find evidence, but she wanted to do whatever she could to help.

Irish shifted into Park and climbed down from his pickup.

Before he could round the front of the truck, Tessa had pushed open her door. Yet she sat in the passenger seat, staring at the trail along the river where it disappeared into the stand of trees lining each side. Her body tense and her eyes wide, her breathing came in short, rapid spasms.

Irish touched her arm.

She jumped, her gaze shooting to him.

"Sorry," he said. "I didn't mean to startle you."

She shook her head. "No, it's not you. I'm just jumpy."

"You have every right to be." He held out his hand.

She laid her fingers in his palm. "Let's do this."

"You don't have to be afraid. The sheriff and I will make sure you're protected."

"I know. It's just…so soon after…" She stepped onto the running board and dropped to the ground. When she tipped forward, off balance, Irish wrapped an arm around her waist to steady her.

"Are you okay?" he asked.

"I am," she nodded. "Just incredibly clumsy."

"Can't say that I mind." His voice came out low and rich, his arm tightening around her. The scent of her hair curled around his nostrils and made him drag in a deep breath. She smelled so good.

Irish's jeans tightened. Now was not the time to be so attracted to this woman. She'd been attacked. For all they knew, the perpetrator had been about to rape or kill her.

THE SHERIFF WAITED at the beginning of the trail.

When Tessa and Irish joined him, he turned and fell into step with them. "Do you remember about where the attack occurred?" the sheriff asked.

She nodded. "It's where the weeping willows hang over the trail." The muscles in her belly tightened. An inordinate amount of fear welled up inside. Even when her husband beat her, she hadn't felt this anxious. Probably because she'd known it was coming.

With the attack this morning, she'd been taken off guard. And it had all happened so quickly. Her breaths became shorter and her chest tightened. If she wasn't careful, she'd have a full-on panic attack before they reached the spot.

A large warm hand reached for hers, gently wrapping around her cold fingers. That little bit of connection was enough to slow her pulse and bring her back from the edge.

Tessa glanced up at Irish.

He gave her an almost imperceptible nod and then focused on the trail ahead.

That's what she needed to do. Focus.

Her footsteps faltered as they approached the willows bending toward the trail, not quite touching. What once had provided a welcome respite from the hot Texas sun now represented a more sinister place.

A shiver rippled down the back of Tessa's neck.

The sheriff bent to examine the ground, pointing at the dusty trail. "We have a good shoe print here. It's a lot bigger than yours. It could belong to your attacker.

Irish's hand squeezed hers. "I was out here earlier, but those treads don't match my running shoes."

"No. They look more like some kind of hiking boots." The sheriff pulled his cell phone out of his pocket and snapped pictures of the print. "Did either of you see any others while you were jogging?"

Tessa stared at the boot print. "I rarely see anyone, except Irish."

"Same," Irish said. "We've been passing each other most mornings and I haven't seen anyone else on the trail at the time we come."

"You keep the same schedule every day?" the sheriff asked.

Irish and Tessa nodded simultaneously.

"I actually should know better," Irish said. "When deployed to a foreign country, we have to vary our schedules and break up habits to keep from becoming targets."

Tessa shook her head. "But we're not in a foreign country. We're in Texas."

"But the same precautions should be taken."

"Things like this aren't supposed to happen in small towns," Tessa said.

"They happen more often than you'd think," the sheriff said, his tone serious.

Tessa shivered. "I moved home to get away from the big city and the crime that goes along with it. But mostly to get away from my ex-husband."

The sheriff's mouth twisted. "We do the best we can. However, we can't read the minds of criminals. Our jobs would be a lot easier if we could."

"I know." Tessa touched the sheriff's arm. "It's just frightening to know that this type of evil is free and walking among us. Who will he attack next?"

"I don't have much to go on, other than your account and description. I'll poke around here and see if I can find anything else that could lead us to the perp."

"Thanks, Sheriff." Irish pulled Tessa's hand through the crook of his elbow. "I'll take Miss Bolton back to Whiskey Gulch."

"I'll let you know if I discover anything," the sheriff offered.

"Thank you," Tessa murmured. *Just find him.*

Irish walked her back to his truck and helped her into the cab. He paused and looked up at her before closing the door. "Are you going to be okay?"

She nodded, a sob rising her throat. Tessa swallowed hard to push it back down. Irish was just being nice. "Thank you."

He climbed into the truck and started the engine. "For what?"

"For believing me and for bringing me back here so that I didn't have to face it alone."

Irish pulled out onto the highway and drove to Whiskey Gulch, a frown tugging his brow downward. When he pulled up in front of the sheriff's office next to her vehicle, he shifted into Park, climbed out and hurried to the passenger side.

Tessa fumbled with her seat belt.

"Here, let me," he said and reached around her to unsnap the buckle, leaning close to her in the process.

Tessa inhaled the scent of him, all warm and woodsy from having jogged along the same trail that morning. She wanted to reach out and smooth a hand over his taut muscles. Were they as hard as they appeared?

The thought came on so swiftly, her hand rose from her lap before she could think straight.

"Are you sure you're all right?" he asked. Still inside the cab with her, he was so close, Tessa could have leaned forward ever so slightly and kissed him.

Her eyes rounded and her breaths came in shallow, constricted gulps. "Yes. Yes, of course."

Irish leaned back out of the truck and offered her his hand. "I could stay with you today, if you like," he offered.

Tessa took his hand and let him help her down. "That won't be necessary. I work all day and I'm surrounded by people." She gave him a weak smile. "I'll be fine."

"What about tonight?" he asked, his tone softening.

"I'll be fine. I get home before sunset and I'll be sure to check all dark corners to make sure there isn't anyone lurking."

"Is your house near others?" Irish asked.

Tessa shrugged. "Somewhat. I'm at the end of a street, if that's what you mean."

"That doesn't mean you're surrounded by other houses."

"I have a house on one side," she said.

"And across the street?" he prompted.

Her lips pressed together. "Empty lot."

Irish's brows knit. "I'll come over and check your house when you get off work."

She shook her head. Since divorcing her husband, she'd been determined to make it on her own, guarding her independence with a vengeance. Though it would be nice to have some backup in this case.

Tessa exhaled the deep breath she'd taken at his words. "That's not necessary. I've lived on my own. I know the drill. Have my key ready before I get out of the car. Look in all directions before leaving the relative safety of the vehicle. I even have a small can of Mace on my keychain."

Irish crossed his arms over his chest. "How long have you had the Mace?"

"About three years. I bought it in Houston."

"That stuff might have a limited shelf life."

"If it makes you feel better, I'll check the date on it." She touched his arm. "I'll be fine."

His eyes narrowing, Irish stared at her for a long time. Then he held out his hand. "Let me have your cell phone."

"My cell phone?" Tessa frowned.

With a nod, Irish wiggled his fingers. "Your cell phone."

Tessa reached into her SUV and pulled her cell out of the cup holder, then she gave it to Irish.

He held it out. "Unlock it."

She entered her code and pushed the phone back to him.

Irish added himself to her contacts and passed it back to her. "Now you have my phone number. If for any reason you're scared, bored or lonely, call me." He curled her fingers around the phone and squeezed gently. "I'm not just saying that to be nice. I really mean it. If you hear something go bump in the night, call me. I'll be there." He scowled. "I don't like the idea of you being alone in your house after what happened."

She touched his arm. "You don't have to worry about me. I'm not your responsibility."

His scowl deepened. "I know that, but I also know what happened to you today. I'm worried about you."

"I'll be okay."

"At least let me follow you home and make sure no one is lurking around your place."

Her lips twisted for a brief moment and then she sighed. "Okay. If it will make you feel better."

Irish nodded. "It would."

Tessa didn't want to admit she was relieved that someone would follow her to her house. Though she tried to sound tough, she wasn't feeling at all safe. She'd been attacked in broad daylight. It could happen again.

A shiver rippled down the center of her spine. "Do you have time to follow me now?" she asked. "I need to get to my house, change and go to work."

Irish nodded. "I'll be right behind you." He held her door for her as she slid behind the steering wheel of her vehicle. Once he'd closed the door, he hurried for his truck and climbed into the driver's seat.

Tessa waited for him to back out of his parking space before she pulled out onto Main Street and headed toward her house.

Her attacker had gotten away. What if he came after her again?

She checked her rearview mirror several times during the few blocks to her house. Still shaken, she was glad Irish was behind her.

Chapter Three

Irish pulled into the driveway beside Tessa's SUV and stared at the little quaint and homey sky-blue cottage with the white shutters.

He quickly shifted into Park and shut off the engine. Jumping out, he came around to her driver's-side door as she pushed it open. "Key?"

Before exiting the vehicle, Tessa stared hard at her home. "Do you really think he might come looking for me here?"

"Since you don't know who he is, or why he attacked you, it pays to be overly cautious. Let me check things out before you go inside."

She nodded and laid the keys across his open palm.

When her fingers touched his skin, he felt a jolt of awareness blast through him. She wasn't the usual kind of woman he found himself dating. She was far too serious and had that girl-next-door thing going on with her strawberry-blond hair and blue-gray eyes.

"Stay here and lock the doors."

Tessa shivered. "What about you? What if there is someone inside? You could be hurt."

He gave her a tight smile. "I'm a trained combatant. I've done this before."

"That's right. You were Special Forces." She shrugged. "I'll stay here." She pulled her cell phone out of her purse. "I'll be ready to call 9-1-1 if you're not back in less than three minutes."

He chuckled. "Good thinking. If the house is empty, I'll be back in less time." He leaned in and kissed her cheek.

Tessa touched the spot he'd kissed, her eyes wide. "Why did you do that?"

"For luck." He winked. "If it bothered you, I won't do it again."

"No. It's okay." She looked down at her hands "It just surprised me."

"Sorry." He tipped his head toward her steering wheel. "If you have to, leave and go back to the sheriff's office." Irish closed her door. "Lock it."

After she did, he climbed the steps to the front porch and checked the doorknob.

Locked. That was good.

He inserted the key into the lock and opened the door, slowly. He hadn't brought his handgun with him. Hopefully, he wouldn't need it.

Pushing the door open, he peered inside. The front entry was shaded from the morning sun. Stepping in, he stood for a moment, listening for sounds, waiting until his vision adjusted to the dim lighting.

One by one, he moved from room to room, checking in closets, underneath beds, behind the shower curtain and in the pantry. There wasn't a basement or garage, so he was done in under three minutes and back out on the porch. "All clear."

Before he could get to her SUV, Tessa had the door open and was getting out.

Irish cupped her elbow. "Sure you're feeling okay?"

She nodded. "I'm fine. Just a little shaky. I didn't expect to get attacked on my morning run."

"No one expects that. You should really have a running buddy, never go on your own."

"I don't know many avid runners. Most people are too busy with young families to get out that early in the morning."

"I'll run with you," Irish said. "There is such a thing as safety in numbers."

The corners of Tessa's mouth dropped. "I hate that I have to rely on anyone. I fought hard for my independence. I feel like it's being stripped away from me."

He held up his hands. "I have no intention of taking away your independence. But it would be unwise to run alone. Especially after what happened today."

She agreed. "I know that, now." Her frown deepened. "I don't like it. But I know it." She sighed. "Thank you. I can start earlier to match your usual time."

"Fair enough. And having you with me will keep me safe," he said with a crooked grin.

Tessa snorted softly. "Like you need someone to keep you safe."

"Despite popular belief, I'm not indestructible. Neither are you." He stuck out his hand. "Promise you won't stand me up tomorrow morning?"

Tessa placed her hand in his. "I promise."

He smiled. "That wasn't so hard, was it?"

"Harder than you think," she muttered.

He let go of her hand and took her other one in his, holding it firmly. "Ready?"

She drew in a deep breath and let it out slowly. "My knees are shaking," she confessed.

He laughed and squeezed her hand. "Mine do that after a good hard run. It goes away."

"I know that feeling. But this is different."

"I'm sure it is," he said.

She shook her head and stood staring at the house. "What's wrong with me? I've entered this house alone many times. This is my home. I shouldn't be afraid to go inside."

Irish hated seeing the fear in her face. He let go of her hand and slipped his arm around her waist. "I'm with you every step of the way. The house is clear. No one inside to jump out at you."

"I trust you," she admitted. "I'm just a bit punchy, is all."

"One step at a time is all you need." He waited for her to take that first step.

And she did. Followed by another and another. Soon, they had climbed the steps to the front porch.

Irish had left the front door open. "You want me to go first?" he asked.

She nodded. "Please."

He took her hand again and led the way inside. "I'll stay as long as you like. Or you can tell me to leave and I'll wait outside."

"I really thought I could handle this on my own. But now I'm not so sure." She squeezed his hand. "Stay."

"I checked all the closets, under the bed and in the pantry. No bogeymen hiding anywhere in the house." He smiled down at her. "You'll be all right."

"I know," Tessa said.

He hated seeing her so afraid of walking into her home. Irish wanted to find the bastard who'd done this to Tessa. The attack had stripped her of any kind of feeling of safety, even in her own home.

He'd talk with Trace. Maybe there was something they could do to help. At the very least, Irish planned to be with her as much as possible to ensure the attacker didn't get a second chance.

TESSA STARED AT the interior of her little cottage. Everything looked just like it had when she'd left it that morning to go jog. Everything inside the house was the same, except for the woman standing in the doorway with a man she barely knew.

Irish stood beside her. "I'll leave you here." His fingers loosened around hers.

Tessa tightened her hold on his hand, suddenly reluctant to let go of his warmth and strength.

"Or not." He chuckled. "Take your time, but I can't hold your hand while you dress for work." A teasing grin tipped his lips. "Unless you want me to." He shook his head. "At the very least, I'll be here until you're ready to go to work. Then I'll follow you there."

She let go of his hand. "Are you sure?"

He nodded.

"You need to get to work, too."

He chortled. "The horses can wait. While you're getting dressed, I'll call Trace and let him know what's going on."

Tessa rubbed her arms as if chilled. "I don't know what's wrong with me. I've walked through my front door a hundred times and never felt like this."

Irish touched her arm. "You've never been attacked like that before. You have a right to feel nervous. But I'm here. I've got your six. You can do this."

"You're right. I can do this." Tessa squared her shoulders and marched toward her bedroom door. As she reached the threshold, she glanced over her shoulder at the man standing in the entryway.

He gave her a nod.

Tessa entered her bedroom, closed the door behind her and leaned against the cool wood panel. A rush of emotions washed over her. Allowing herself a couple minutes to fall apart, she shook from head to toe. Then she stood tall, willed steel into her spine, gathered her scrubs and underwear and headed into the adjoining bathroom. Maybe if she washed away the dirt from the trail, she'd feel more like herself—the cool, confident nurse who had it together.

Inside the bathroom, she grabbed the shower curtain, her heart hammering against the wall of her chest. Then she released the curtain and let go of a strangled laugh. As Irish had promised, no one was hiding in the shower or anywhere else in the house.

Feeling a bit ridiculous, Tessa stripped out of her workout clothes and stepped beneath the spray, letting the warm water wash away the grit and grime she'd acquired from rolling in the gravel along the river road. The bandage Irish had applied to her knee soaked off, allowing water to clean the scrape. It stung, reminding Tessa that she was alive, not left to die beside the river. She'd used her skills and brain to get herself out of the situation.

Squirting shampoo into her hands, she rubbed it into her scalp and rinsed. Then she put dab of body-wash on her loofa and scrubbed every inch of skin, erasing the feel of her attacker's hands on her body.

As the dirt from the trail washed down the drain, Tessa thought about the man standing outside her bedroom door, waiting for her to finish dressing for work.

She'd thought about him on a number of days as he'd jogged by her. Tessa had wondered who he was and what his story was. At the very least, she knew he was honorable and that he would never do what the attacker had done. Call it a gut feeling, she knew Irish was a good man.

Determined not to take any more time than she had to, she rinsed off, applied conditioner to her hair and rinsed all over. After switching off the water, she climbed out of the shower and toweled dry.

She ran a brush through her wet hair then slipped into her undergarments and scrubs. The woman staring back at her from the mirror was the Tessa she knew and was familiar with, not the scared woman who'd entered the bathroom a few minutes before.

With little time to spare to get to work, and not wanting to keep Irish any longer than she had to, she pulled her hair back into a tight ponytail and wrapped the tail into a bun at the nape of her neck.

It was still wet, but that was okay. With the warm Texas weather, her hair would dry quickly.

She cast another glance at her reflection. With her hair pulled back from her face, the bruise on her temple was more apparent. She thought about applying concealer to the bruise, but that would take too much time.

She didn't care if people saw the bruise. Someone had attacked her. Wasn't it best for folks to know an attacker was out there so they could take precautions and not suffer her same fate or worse?

Tessa slipped into her shoes and left her bedroom.

Irish had his back to her, staring out the front window of her cottage. He turned to see her standing there staring at him.

Heat rose up her neck, flooding her cheeks.

"Ready?" he asked.

She nodded. "Almost. I'd like to make a sandwich to take for lunch."

"Take your time. I called Trace. He said he'd get started feeding the animals."

Tessa grabbed her purse. "I can skip the sandwich. Let's get on the road. I've already taken up too much of your time. I don't want to hold you up any longer."

Irish smiled. "You're not holding me up. I promise." He tilted his head toward her kitchen. "Come on, let's make your sandwich. What do you usually have?"

She followed him into the kitchen. "I throw a bit of deli turkey, tomato and lettuce on a couple slices of bread. But peanut butter and jelly will hold me over a twelve-hour shift."

Irish shook his head. "No way. Come on, I'll make your sandwich." He headed for the refrigerator. "Everything in all the usual places?"

She nodded. "Yes. But I can make my own sandwich. You don't have to."

"Allow me." He opened the refrigerator and fished out the lettuce, tomatoes, turkey and mayonnaise.

Tessa tore off a paper towel and laid two slices of bread on top of it.

Irish quickly assembled the sandwich.

"I really am quite capable of making my own lunch," she said.

Irish grinned. "I get that. This gives me something to do and keeps me out of trouble."

"Can I get you some coffee?" she asked. "I'm making some for myself."

"Sure," he said. "I'd like that."

While she made coffee, he wrapped her sandwich in cellophane. They worked side by side in the small kitchen.

Tessa was surprised at how naturally they moved around each other. Her ex-husband would never have helped her make a sandwich for himself, much less her.

He'd never bothered to do anything around the house. The kitchen, especially, was woman's work and her responsibility. She'd been happy to work there. Randy rarely entered it, if only to grab a beer from the refrigerator.

Her husband had always found fault in everything Tessa did. Cooking had been one of Tessa's escapes, the kitchen a sanctuary from his criticism.

By the time Tessa had two steaming cups of coffee ready, Irish had the sandwich wrapped and tucked into her insulated lunch bad along with a package of potato chips.

She snapped lids on top of the travel mugs of coffee and handed Irish one of them.

He held out the lunch bag. "Ready?"

Tessa nodded. "Ready."

"Let's go," he said. "I'll follow you to the hospital."

"Really, you don't have to follow me. I can get there on my own. Nobody is going to attack me in a moving vehicle."

"Call me overly cautious," Irish said. "I want to

see you all the way to the hospital and inside the door before I turn you loose." He frowned. "Humor me."

She gave him a weak smile. "I really do appreciate what you're doing for me. I should get my act together."

"Lady," Irish said, "your act is together. You're holding up better than any female I've known—or male, for that matter—after being attacked like you were."

They left the cottage together.

Irish locked the door and handed her the keys.

Irish escorted her to her SUV, opened the door and inspected the inside before he allowed her to get in.

Maybe it was overkill, but it made Tessa feel better, knowing there wasn't someone waiting to pounce on her. Eventually, she'd have to check her house and car on her own.

Tessa valued her independence and guarded it fiercely after she'd left Randy, knowing she'd be on her own. Now that she was safe from the man who'd verbally and physically abused her, she was exposed to others who might harm her, such as the one person who'd attacked her on the trail.

For six months, she'd lived in the bubble of the little town of Whiskey Gulch, going about her life, lulled into a sense of peace and belonging. Small towns were supposed to be safe, weren't they? After this morning, Tessa wasn't sure.

She slipped in behind the wheel of her SUV.

"Lock the door," Irish commanded from outside her window.

Tessa clicked the button. The lock snapped into place. She pulled the seat belt around her and clicked the buckle.

Had it really been only that morning since she'd been attacked? It felt like a day ago, or maybe a week…so much had happened in between. Now she was on her way to work, like any other day.

Tessa backed out of her driveway and pulled out onto the street.

Irish followed close behind, all the way to the hospital.

She pulled into her usual spot and waited while Irish parked his truck in the space next to hers and got out.

He came around his vehicle to open the door to her SUV.

"I think I can take it from here," she insisted.

He held out his hand. "Once you're inside the doors."

She sighed. "I hate that I feel like a toddler being dropped off at the day care."

He chuckled. "Not even close." Irish held out his arm for her and waited while she decided how far she was willing to take his protector side.

"I have to do this by myself," she said. "It's daylight. The parking lot is populated. I can get myself from my car to the building without any problem."

"Again," he said with a twist to his lips, "humor

me. I feel better knowing that you're inside the hospital and safe."

Tessa clamped her lips shut to keep from arguing about his insistent involvement.

When they reached the entrance to the emergency room, the automatic doors opened and her coworker, Allison Wade, spotted her from where she sat at the administration desk.

"Tessa, sweetie." Allison hurried over, grabbed Tessa's arm and drew her through the entrance and into the ER lobby. "I heard about what happened." She scanned her from head to toe. "Are you all right?"

Tessa glanced over her shoulder at Irish and gave him a little wave. "How many people know?"

"We all heard." Allison led Tessa through the restricted doors and into the tiny break room. "Brian was on duty at the fire station when the call came out over the police scanner. He called me as soon as he knew it was you." Allison glanced toward the other nurses and doctors coming through the door.

"And Allison let us all know," said Dr. Slade, the ER doctor on duty.

Tessa guffawed. "Good news travels fast, doesn't it?"

"Good news?" Allison shook her head. "I was terrified for you."

Dr. Slade pulled out his pen light and shone it into Tessa's eyes. "That's a nasty bruise you have."

"I'm fine," Tessa said. "He hit me there."

The doctor winced. "We should do a thorough once-over to make sure you aren't missing anything."

"No, really, Dr. Slade. Everything is where it should be." Tessa held up her hands. "Other than the bruise and a few scrapes on my knees, I'm okay. I got away before he did any real damage."

"At least let me get an ice pack for that bruise." Allison headed for the supply cabinet.

"No, Allison," Tessa said, pushing through the crush of staff members. "We have work to do."

"Work, schmerk," Allison said. "I'm getting that ice pack." She led Tessa to the supply cabinet, grabbed a cool pack and pressed it to Tessa's face. "Here, hold that against your temple while I take care of a patient."

"Look," Tessa said. "I'm here to work. I'm perfectly capable of manning my shift. This little bruise on the side of my face is nothing."

"Yeah," Allison said. "And being attacked on a lonely road is nothing. I don't think so. I'd be terrified to leave my house."

Tessa couldn't refute Allison's words when she'd been afraid to go into her house, much less come back out. If it hadn't been for Irish, she might have been more hesitant to get back out…but she would have. Life went on. "Really," she said. "I'm okay." Her statement was as much for herself as for Allison.

Allison nodded. "Okay. But at least tell me who the hunk was who brought you to work. Tell me you got his number."

Tessa's cheeks heated. "That's Irish. He works out

at Whiskey Gulch Ranch and runs every morning along the river, a little earlier than I do."

Allison grinned. "Do they have more hunks like him out at the ranch? Is Irish single? Tell me all."

"You have a boyfriend." Tessa shook her head. "What about Brian?"

Allison's grin widened. "Brian and I have been together so long, we could stand a little competition."

Tessa shrugged. "I really don't know much about Irish, other than he likes to jog in the morning."

"How did he end up following you to work?" Allison asked.

"He was at the sheriff's office when I came skidding in sideways after the attack. He's been with me ever since, just to make sure I'm okay."

Allison scrunched her nose. "He runs when you run? Are you sure he wasn't the one who attacked you?"

Tessa shook her head. "No way. He was already in town when I was still out jogging. Besides, the man who attacked me was heavier set than Irish and bigger around the middle."

Allison tipped her head. "I don't know. Irish is pretty tall and broad-shouldered."

Tessa's heart fluttered. "Yes, he is."

Allison took Tessa's hands. "If you need a place to stay for a few days, you can stay in my apartment. I have a spare bedroom you can sleep in until the guy is caught."

"Not necessary," Tessa said. "I have a can of Mace in my purse and a handgun in my nightstand."

Allison cocked an eyebrow. "And you know how to use both?"

"Damn right I do," Tessa responded.

"That's my girl." Allison hugged Tessa.

"All right," Tessa said. "Let's get to work."

Working helped settle her nerves…some. All day long, she looked over her shoulder and jumped when someone touched her arm. She studied every man she came into contact with, wondering if the attacker was walking among them.

Physically and emotionally exhausted by the end of her shift, she wasn't surprised her head throbbed and her back ached. She hadn't taken a break, afraid she'd think too much if she didn't stay busy.

"Hey, Tessa," Allison called out behind her as she organized another drawer of supplies.

Tessa turned. "Shouldn't you be on your way home?"

Allison glanced at the clock on the wall. "Yes. And so should you. The offer still stands. You can come home with me and stay until they catch your attacker."

Tessa shook her head. "I can't do that. We don't know when or if they'll find the guy. I'm sure you don't want me moving in with you indefinitely."

Allison shrugged. "I'm okay with that. Or I could move in with you. As long as you don't mind Brian coming over every night." She winked.

"Really, I'm all right. I'll be fine," Tessa said and closed the drawer she'd finished.

Allison stood with one fist perched on her hip. "Then why haven't you left yet?" She cocked an eyebrow.

Tessa sighed. "I needed to fix the supply cabinet and drawers. They were a mess."

"They're always a mess." Allison took her arm. "I'll follow you home, if it will make you feel better." She walked with her to the exit.

As the glass door slid open, a familiar face appeared on the other side.

Tessa's heart fluttered.

"Never mind," Allison murmured. "Your bodyguard has arrived."

Irish stood on the sidewalk outside the hospital, a grin on his face.

Tessa's cheeks filled with heat. "What are you doing here?"

His grin twisted. "Not a '*Gee, Irish, I'm so glad to see you*'?" He nodded toward Allison. "I'll take her from here."

Allison batted her eyes and smiled. "I'm sure she's in good hands." She let go of Tessa's arm and waved. "See you in the morning." And she left Tessa standing in front of Irish, feeling very much like she'd been cast adrift in a riptide.

Irish held out his hand. "Do you want to ride with me, or will you be driving your own car?"

She had to think before she could respond. The man made her head spin. Or was that the residual bump on her temple or the headache that had been nagging her all day? Whatever… "I'll drive mine," she told him. "But you don't—"

He held up his hand. "You might want to save it. I'm following you, either way."

Tessa let out a breath. She wouldn't admit aloud that she was glad to see him and going home wasn't nearly as scary with Irish watching her six.

So much for being an independent divorcée.

Chapter Four

Irish had spent the day worrying about Tessa. He hadn't liked leaving her side, even though she'd been at the hospital all day, surrounded by people.

With her attacker at large, Tessa wasn't safe. He might already be plotting his next opportunity to surprise her when she least expected it.

He escorted Tessa to her SUV and held the door for her.

"Thank you," she said as she slid into the driver's seat.

He grinned. "My pleasure."

After he closed her door, he hurried to his truck and waited for her to pull out onto the street.

The drive to her house didn't take long. His plan was to stay with her as long as she'd let him. The woman was hardheaded and determined to handle the situation on her own. He'd brought reinforcements to help his cause.

Dinner.

Tessa pulled into her driveway and parked.

He wished her little cottage had a garage she

could park in and close the door before she got out of her vehicle. Then again, anyone determined enough could slip into the garage as she closed the door. Then she'd be trapped in the garage with him, and no one would know.

Irish studied the location, not liking it at all. Hers was the last house on the street with an empty lot across from her. The one house on the other side appeared to be closed up and the one diagonal from hers had a For Sale sign out front.

From what he could tell, she was alone on her street. If she screamed for help, no one would hear.

All the more reason to stay, Irish told himself.

Not that she'd let him.

Thus the pizza he'd ordered before he left the Whiskey Gulch Ranch and picked up on the way through town. Who could resist a pizza with all the best toppings?

His mouth watered at the scent of cheese, to-mato sauce and pepperoni. If she didn't like all the fixin's, he had the backup. A chicken salad with several choices of dressings—chicken on the side in case she was vegan.

He'd borrowed a chick flick from Rosalyn Travis, his boss's mother.

The longer he could convince Tessa to let him stay, the better he'd feel. The thought of leaving her alone made his skin crawl.

Irish climbed out of his truck, grabbed the pizza, salad and video, and met Tessa as she exited her ve-hicle. "I don't suppose you like pizza and salad?"

She lifted her nose and sniffed. "Pepperoni?"

He nodded. "And everything else but anchovies."

She closed her eyes and her lips slipped into a smile. "Sounds amazing."

"Rosalyn Travis sent a romantic comedy movie. Said something about cheering you up." So, it was a little lie. The movie had been Irish's idea. He'd asked Mrs. Travis for a funny chick flick that would help take Tessa's mind off the attack.

"That was very thoughtful of her." Tessa closed her SUV door and pressed the lock button on her key fob. The locks clicked in place. "Please tell her thank you. She's always so kind when I run into her in town."

"I think she's adopted all of us as her children. Her husband's death was pretty hard on her."

"Having Trace home from the military seems to have made a difference."

Irish nodded. "He's a good guy. Always had our backs when we deployed."

Tessa walked toward the cottage, her key in hand. "Everyone in town was surprised to learn that Matt Hennessy was Mr. Travis's son from a previous relationship before he married Rosalyn."

"No more surprised than Matt and Trace."

"How's that co-ownership of the Whiskey Gulch Ranch going?"

"Matt and Trace are great to work for." Irish shook his head. "They couldn't be more different, and yet have the same philosophies and values." He balanced the pizza box in one hand. "If you'll unlock the door, I'll clear the interior before you go in."

Thankfully, she didn't argue this time. The dark circles beneath her eyes told the story. She was too tired to argue.

Carrying the pizza, salad and movie, Irish entered the cottage, senses on alert. In minutes, he'd checked the premises and was back at the front door for Tessa. "All clear."

"Good, because I'm starving and my mouth is watering for that pizza."

Irish held the door as Tessa entered and set her purse on the table in the small foyer.

"I put the pizza on the counter in the kitchen. You can have the whole thing by yourself. If you feel all right with me staying for a bit, I'd love to join you." He smiled. "Your choice. I don't want to crowd you."

"It's your pizza," she said. "You should stay and eat it. Unless you need to leave, in which case, I'd love to grab a slice before you go."

"I'm kind of new in town. I don't have anywhere else I have to be." He closed and locked the door. "Point me to the paper plates."

"All the animals are fed?" Tessa entered the kitchen and pulled plates from the cabinet.

"All fed. The stalls have been mucked and I even had time to shower." He winked. "I hear some women love the earthy scent of horse manure." He shrugged. "I don't get it. But whatever melts their butter."

Tessa laughed. "Thank you for showering. I, for

one, prefer to eat without the earthy scent of horse manure mixing with the delicious aroma of pizza sauce and cheese."

Irish opened the pizza box and stood back for her to choose first. "Then I made a wise choice and we have something else in common."

"And what do we have in common?" she asked as she selected a slice of pizza.

"We like pepperoni and jogging in the morning."

Her hand holding the pizza stopped halfway to her mouth.

Irish could have kicked himself for bringing up the subject of jogging. He was there to help her *forget* about the incident, not to remind her. At least for a little while. "I'm sorry. I shouldn't—"

She shook her head. "No. Don't. I have to get back out there and jog again. I don't want my running to be the trigger that makes me afraid to get outside. I worked too hard to get to the point I am to let the…assault…set me back." She squared her shoulders and took a bite of the pizza. "Mmm." Her eyes closed for a moment and her face appeared euphoric. "So good."

Irish almost choked on the bite of pizza he'd taken at the same time.

Her moans and the way her chest rose and fell made him think of other things that could make a woman moan and breath heavily besides eating pizza.

His groin tightened and he fought to swallow the

wad of pizza at the back of his throat. When it caught instead, he coughed.

Tessa set her pizza on a plate and pounded his back. "Do I need to perform the Heimlich maneuver?"

Tears ran from his eyes as he shook his head. "Wrong pipe," he managed to choke out.

She pulled a beer from the refrigerator, twisted off the top and handed it to him. "Wash it down."

He took the bottle and upended it, sluicing the pizza down his throat. When he could breathe again, he sighed. "Thank you." He checked the bottle and grinned. "We have another thing in common…we like the same beer."

She smiled. "Good." Tessa got another beer from the fridge, opened it and took a long swallow. "I don't like drinking alone."

"That's why you have me here," Irish said. "With pizza, salad and a movie guaranteed to make you laugh, what more could you ask for?"

"Peace of mind. Never being attacked again. Never having to worry whether I'll live to see another day?" She carried her plate and beer into the living room and sat on one end of the sofa.

Irish shoved the salad into the refrigerator and followed Tessa into the living room with his plate of pizza and the movie. "That's pretty heavy thinking."

"Which could lead to some pretty heavy drinking." She took another sip of her beer and stared at the bottle. "But I need a relatively clear head in case he comes back to finish what he started." Tessa set the bottle on the coffee table and took another bite of pizza.

Irish held up the movie. "Ready for some entertainment to get your mind off less pleasant musings?"

Tessa nodded. "Sure." She rose and took the movie from him.

When their hands touched, a spark of electricity zipped through Irish.

A soft gasp escaped Tessa's lips.

Irish glanced up.

Tessa's eyes flared. She jerked the movie from his grasp and clutched it to her breast. Without uttering a word, she spun, darted to the television, and fumbled to open the movie's case.

Once she had the disc in the player, she grabbed her plate and carried it to the kitchen.

"You're not done, are you?" Irish asked.

"No," she said. "I'm going back for more."

More.

That's exactly what Irish wanted. More.

But not pizza.

Music poured from the speaker and the movie introductions flashed on the screen.

Tessa, with her plate and a second slice of pizza, settled on the other end of the couch. Just out of Irish's reach.

That was probably for the best. If Tessa sat too close, Irish would be tempted to put his arm around her and pull her close. He blamed the urge to hold her on his need to protect her, nothing else.

But that wasn't the truth. He'd been drawn to this woman with the athletic build, strawberry-blond hair and gray-blue eyes since the first day he'd come across her jogging the river trail. She'd flashed him a shy smile and kept running.

That smile had made his day when he'd been so new in town. She'd warmed him with the simple gesture and made him think of Whiskey Gulch as home.

Which was what he'd wanted all along. A place to call home. He'd left the military to start a new life. Actually, to start living a normal life, where he wasn't gone from home the majority of the year and he could come home to dinner most nights.

Granted, he came home to an empty apartment and frozen dinners unless Rosalyn Travis invited him to eat with their family. Rosalyn, with her son's fiancée could cook up a helluva a meal, enough to feed an army, if needed.

And Irish repaid them by volunteering to wash dishes and occasionally grill steaks in the backyard.

Tessa adjusted the volume on the movie to a low, steady hum they could hear without being blasted out of the small living room.

Irish found himself watching Tessa more than the movie, wanting to know more about this woman who'd fought her way free of an attacker. He was impressed.

Irish's lips quirked. "Your self-defense lessons really paid off."

She glanced his way and nodded.

"Why did you think Whiskey Gulch would be

such a rough place to live you'd need lessons on how to defend yourself in order to live here?"

Tessa's gaze shifted from him to the wall and she shrugged. "I had my reasons."

"Were you worried about anyone besides your ex-husband?" Irish leaned forward. "Perhaps we should start by questioning him."

Tessa disagreed, telling him, "No, I wasn't worried about anyone here. Otherwise, I would have been more aware and watchful during my morning runs."

"A woman can't be too careful these days," Irish said.

"Especially when the one hitting her is someone she knows," Tessa murmured.

"Sadly, that's true." Irish's hands clenched into fists, anger burning deep in his chest.

"It's not important." Tessa didn't look his way. Her gaze remained firmly on the romantic comedy neither one of them had been watching.

"It sure as hell is!" Irish exclaimed. "If your ex-husband did this, he needs to be stopped. Did you tell the sheriff about him? He might be the one who attacked you today."

"I doubt it," Tessa said. "He works and lives in San Antonio."

"And you know he's in San Antonio? It's only a couple of hours away by road. Faster if he flies."

She waved her hand. "He wouldn't take the time to come after me. And I have a restraining order against him. He only hit me when it was convenient for him to do so."

Irish snorted. "When is it ever convenient to hit a woman?"

"When you're married to her?" Tessa chose that moment to look at Irish. "He was my husband. He thought he had every right to hit me."

Irish's hands clenched into fists. "No man has the right to hit any woman," he said through gritted teeth.

Tessa's lips formed a firm line and she lifted her chin. "I came to the same conclusion. After he put me in the hospital, I filed for divorce, took self-defense classes and then moved home to Whiskey Gulch. I couldn't get far enough, fast enough."

"Oh, Tessa…" Irish reached across the gap between them and took her hand. "I'm sorry."

"For what?" She stared down at his hand holding hers but didn't pull it free. "You didn't hit me."

"I'm sorry that you went through that and then had it happen to you again this morning." He lifted her hand and pressed his lips to the backs of her knuckles. "I wish I'd been there for you. If I'd been a few minutes later…"

"Or if I'd been a few minutes earlier." She curled her fingers around his. "He might have waited for another day, another time and caught me just as unaware." Tessa squeezed his hand and let go. "The point is… I'm okay. Now, I'm aware and it won't happen again." She pushed to her feet. "I'm tired and need to get some sleep before my shift tomorrow."

Irish rose. "And our jog before that?"

"And our jog before that," she agreed with a smile.

"I don't like leaving you alone."

"I've been alone since I got back to Whiskey Gulch. I know what to do to stay safe."

"I get that you need your independence, but I'm worried that jerk will come back."

"I'll leave all the lights on, have my gun beneath my pillow and my Mace with me as well." She gave him a tight smile. "I've got this."

"And you want me to get out of your hair." He dipped his chin. "Gotcha. You have my phone number. If you hear anything go bump in the night, call me. I don't care if it's a cat dumping over your trash can...call me." He glanced around the small living room. "Do you mind if I check all the window and door locks?"

Tessa waved a hand. "Knock yourself out."

Irish made quick work of testing all the locks on the windows and the back door. He stopped in the front entryway. "You're all set. If you want me to stay, I can camp out on the couch. I've slept in worse places."

She shook her head. "I'm going to be fine. I'm prepared."

"I'd feel better if you had a dog," he said. "A big dog. With sharp teeth."

She chuckled. "I'd be more afraid the dog would attack me than a person breaking and entering." Tessa smiled. "I'd hate to shoot the dog. I wouldn't hesitate to shoot the person."

"Okay, then. If you really don't need me…"

"I don't." Tessa opened the front door.

Irish had no other choice but to leave. He couldn't help someone who didn't want to be helped. "I'll see you in the morning." He leaned forward and brushed her forehead with his lips. "I hope you sleep. You can call me if you just want company."

"Thanks. I appreciate all you've done for me today. I can't keep taking advantage of you."

"I wouldn't offer if I didn't care." He backed out the front door. "I'll stay until I hear the lock click," he said.

She nodded. "Good night, Irish."

"Good night." He stood on the front porch while she closed and locked the door.

For a long moment, he continued to stand there, not wanting to leave her alone.

The darkness surrounding the cottage seemed to hold infinite possibilities, none of which Irish liked. Tessa's attacker could be in the shadows at that very moment, waiting for Irish to leave so that he could make his next move. He'd get motion-sensor flood-lights and install them the next day.

Irish forced himself to turn, walk down the steps and climb into his truck. He checked his cell phone to make sure it was on and the volume was turned up in case it rang and Tessa had changed her mind and invited him to come in and stay the night.

The phone didn't ring and Tessa hadn't changed her mind.

For several minutes, Irish remained in his truck in

Tessa's driveway, letting his vision adjust to the darkness. Nothing moved, not even a neighborhood cat.

He could stay in her driveway and sleep in the truck. Tessa wouldn't be happy. She'd been adamant about preserving her independence. After what her husband had done to her, he didn't blame her for wanting to take care of herself. Her ex hadn't done it for her. Why should she trust another man to keep her safe?

He started the engine and backed out of her driveway, his gut knotting the farther away from her he went.

He hoped and prayed she'd be all right. Driving back to the Whiskey Gulch Ranch, he second-guessed leaving her at least a dozen times. She had his number and there was always 9-1-1. She'd be all right.

Then why did Irish have that bad feeling he always got when something awful was about to happen?

Chapter Five

After Irish left, Tessa leaned against the door and drew in a deep breath. Had it really only been that morning that she'd been attacked? Her forehead still tingled over Irish's kiss. A fleeting thought whisked through her mind that she wished he'd kissed her lips instead.

Tessa pressed her fingers to her mouth. What would that have felt like? Why did she care? She wasn't in the market to find a husband replacement for the defective one she'd fought so hard to be done with.

Irish was different. He took the time to make sure she was all right. Randy never would have followed her from her home to work and back. He'd have expected her to get over whatever was bothering her so that she didn't inconvenience him in any way.

Not Irish. He was a gentleman. He'd brought pizza with no expectation of repayment in any form. The kiss on her forehead had been anything but passionate. Nevertheless, the gesture had sent heat rushing through her body, pooling low in her belly.

How she'd wanted him to kiss her lips.

Tessa moaned and pushed away from the door. The shine of his headlights through the front window announced Irish's departure.

For the first few months she'd been back in Whiskey Gulch, Tessa had struggled with loneliness. Her parents had been older when they'd had her and had passed away while she'd lived in San Antonio with Randy. Tessa was glad they hadn't known what Randy was doing to their only child. Everyone from Whiskey Gulch had assumed their marriage was a match made in heaven. The homecoming king and queen belonged together. They were perfect for each other.

Fortunately, her parents had insisted Tessa go to college. She had and majored in nursing. When she'd returned home, Randy had finished his finance degree from Texas A&M and come back to propose to her.

Fairy tale, right?

Wrong.

Her reality couldn't have been farther from the truth. From the day Tessa had said *I do*, Randy had considered her his property to do with as he pleased.

The honeymoon phase lasted a total of one month. They both got jobs and went to work. Tessa went to work for the ICU department of a major hospital. As the new nurse, she was assigned the night shift.

Randy worked during the day and expected her to have supper ready when he came home. He didn't care if she'd pulled a double shift. Dinner had to be ready or he'd shout at her, belittle her work and hit her if she talked back.

Yeah. Marriage hadn't been the happiest time of her life. She'd stuck with it because they hadn't seen each other much; she'd even volunteered for the night shift to avoid being at home with Randy as much as possible.

Even though Irish had gone around the house checking all the locks, doors and windows, Tessa made another pass once again checking all the latches on the windows, testing the doors to make sure nobody could get in. At each window, she stared out into the night. Every shadow that moved made her jump. The wind ruffling the branches of the trees became specters in the darkness.

She doubted she'd get much sleep that night. If she wasn't so afraid of actually going to sleep, she might consider taking a sleep aid. That wouldn't be good. All she needed was to be sound asleep because of a highly effective sleep aid and have somebody break into her house. She wouldn't wake in time to defend herself. Before morning, she could be raped and dead.

Not for the first time, she thought she needed a dog. A big dog. Or better yet, a bodyguard. One like Irish. Wasn't that what he'd said Travis was setting up? A security business. As in security of persons like her?

Tessa wondered what it would cost to hire a bodyguard. She snorted. As a one-income household, she could barely afford her mortgage payment and utilities. There was no way she had the funds to pay for a bodyguard. Not to mention, Irish hadn't asked to be her bodyguard. He had just assigned himself. For which Tessa was grateful.

When she was satisfied that all the doors and windows were secured, she headed for the bathroom, stripped out of her clothes and pulled on her favorite pajamas. No nightgown for her. If she needed to make a fast getaway, she wanted to make sure she was sufficiently covered.

Anger blossomed in her chest. She shouldn't have to worry about things like this. What kind of animal attacked a defenseless female?

The worst.

Tessa stretched out on her bed, fluffed her pillow and closed her eyes. As soon as she did, flashbacks of the man in the ski mask lunging out of the willow trees whipped through her brain. Her eyes popped open. Maybe she could fall asleep with them open. Yes, that's what she'd do, she'd fall asleep with her eyes open. For the next thirty minutes, she stared at the ceiling, straining to hear every noise. Every creak, every sound, in the house seemed amplified. When she couldn't take it anymore, she picked up her cell phone and dialed Irish's number.

He answered on the second ring. "Hey, beautiful. Miss me already?" he asked.

His warm tones washed over Tessa like a comforting blanket.

"No, I…" she stammered. "I must have accidently dialed you." She hated that she was lying. She hated worse that she felt she'd needed to.

"Having trouble going to sleep?" he asked.

"A little," she admitted.

"I can stay on the line until you go to sleep. I don't mind."

"Are you sure?" she asked.

"I wouldn't offer if I didn't mean it," he said.

"Thank you," she said, and lay there. She allowed her eyes to close. This time she didn't have a flash of her attacker but of Irish jogging toward her on the river trail.

"What shall we talk about?" he asked, his tone deep and rich.

She smiled. "I don't care. Anything."

"How 'bout what's your favorite football team?"

She laughed. "That's easy, the Texas Longhorns."

"No, no, no," he moaned. "You can't be a Longhorn fan."

"Why not?" she asked.

"We can't be together if you're a Longhorn fan, not when I'm an Aggie's supporter."

"That's too bad. And here I thought we were on to something between us. What about the NFL?" she countered.

"Okay, what's your favorite team on the NFL?" he asked.

"Denver Broncos."

He moaned again. "No, no, no, you're from Texas. You're supposed to like the Dallas Cowboys."

"You follow the Cowboys?" she asked.

He chuckled. "Yes, I do. Though they haven't been doing so well this season."

For the next thirty minutes, he talked about his favorite games, the different players, and the best commercials from the past five Super Bowl games.

None of it mattered in the grand scheme of things to Tessa. But just the fact that he was talking to her did. Before long, she was yawning and she must have been loud enough for Irish to hear.

"Are you ready to go to sleep?" he asked.

She nodded even though he couldn't see her. "Yes," she said.

"Sweet dreams, pretty lady," he said.

She smiled with her eyes closed. "Thanks for talking to me."

After the call ended, Tessa lay against the sheets, warm and comfortable, more from the tone of his voice than from the blankets covering her. Soon she drifted into a deep, dreamless sleep.

Seemingly seconds after she'd gone to sleep, the sudden sound of breaking glass jerked her awake. Tessa sat up straight in bed and reached for the gun she'd left lying on the nightstand. Her hands shaking, she flipped the safety switch off and aimed it toward the door. The crunch of broken glass in her kitchen made her slide out of her bed onto the floor on her knees, with the bed between her and the door. She fumbled in the dark for her cell on the nightstand and redialed Irish's number. She didn't know how long she'd been asleep. She prayed that he hadn't gone to sleep himself.

"Please answer," she muttered, "please answer."

Seconds later his voice came on the line. "Tessa, what's wrong?"

"Someone's in my house," she said, her voice low and shaky.

"I'm calling 9-1-1," Irish said. "I'll be there in two minutes. Stay on the line. I'm putting you on hold."

Her hand on the phone shook as she held it to her ear. In her dominant hand, she held her gun, aiming it toward the wooden panel of the door. Sure she knew how to fire the weapon, but normally she went to a gun range and her hands were steady. Right now, she was shaking so badly, she doubted she'd hit anything. Footsteps in the hallway alerted her to the fact that her intruder was headed toward her bedroom.

Two minutes was too long. This guy could get to her before Irish or the sheriff. Summoning enough courage, Tessa shouted, "I know you're there. I have a gun. I will shoot to kill!" The footsteps stopped in the hallway. "The sheriff's on his way."

The doorknob jiggled. Thanking God she'd thought to lock it before she'd gone to bed, Tessa did the only thing she could think to do.

She fired a shot.

It hit square in the middle of the door, going straight through and leaving a small hole.

The wail of sirens sounded in the distance, muffled by the walls of her house.

Again, the doorknob rattled and whoever was in her house kicked the door. By now she could hear the sirens much louder and getting closer. Where was Irish? He said two minutes. Hadn't it been five already? A horn blared over and over and over again. Getting closer and closer to her house. Footsteps in the hallway sounded, racing toward the kitchen. The intruder was on his way out the back. Tessa thought to go after him but thought again. All she needed was to confuse whoever was coming to help her. She might get herself shot by going after the intruder. She hunkered low behind the bed, the gun resting on top of the mattress in case the intruder returned. Her back door slammed open and the footsteps disappeared into the night. Seconds later, she heard pounding on the door.

"Tessa!" Irish's voice called out. "Tessa, open up and let me in."

She hesitated to answer. What if the intruder was waiting for whomever had come to her rescue? What if the intruder shot Irish? Tessa lurched to her feet and ran for her bedroom door, unlocked it and threw it open.

"Look out, Irish! He might still be out there," Tessa shouted. She ran down her hallway, holding her gun in front of her, ready to shoot anyone who stood in her way or who threatened to shoot Irish. When she reached the kitchen, her bare feet landed on a shard of glass and she cried out. A silhouette emerged in the open doorway to her kitchen. Ignoring the sharp pain in her foot, she leveled her gun at the chest of the man standing there in the darkness, her finger resting on the trigger.

"Don't shoot," Irish called out, holding up his hands.

"Oh, thank God." Tessa lowered her gun, a sob rising in her throat.

He flipped on the light switch. "Are you all right?"

She shook her head.

Irish glanced at the kitchen floor and cursed. In seconds, he started across the space between them, glass crunching beneath his boots. "Don't move," he said, his gaze going to her feet on the floor where blood pooled around her heel.

With a shaky laugh, she remained where she stood. "Don't worry. I'm not going anywhere."

When he reached her, he swept her into his arms and carried her into the living room, settling her on the couch. He laid his gun on the coffee table.

"Don't put your gun down. You've got my back," he said. "If anyone comes through that back door, shoot him."

She nodded and held her handgun in her hands, aimed toward the back door. The wail of sirens grew much louder as a sheriff's vehicle pulled into the yard, the lights flashing through the windows.

"I'm going to unlock the front door for the sheriff," he said. "You going to be okay right here?"

She nodded. Just having him in the same room was a relief.

Irish unlocked the front door, threw on the porch light and raised his hands. "Don't shoot," he called out. "I'm the one who called the sheriff's department. Search the perimeter, the intruder might still be around."

"Is Tessa okay?" a female voice called out. Tessa knew that voice. Deputy Dallas Jones, the only female deputy. She was almost as new to Whiskey Gulch as Tessa.

"We might need an ambulance," Irish told Dallas.

"No," Tessa said. "I'm okay. It's just a little cut. I can get to the hospital for stitches if I need them. But I don't need an ambulance."

"Are you sure?" Irish looked at her, his brow furrowed. "It's an awful lot of blood."

"I just need a pair of tweezers and a Band-Aid out of the bathroom in my bedroom. I'm a nurse. This is what I do."

"For other people," Irish pointed out. "You might have a hard time finding the glass in your own foot."

"Okay, I'll let you. If you don't mind? The tweezers are in a drawer in my bathroom. There's a first-aid kit under the sink. If you'll get those, I'd appreciate it."

Irish hurried through her bedroom and into her bathroom and was back in seconds, carrying the first-aid kit, tweezers, a damp washcloth, and a towel. He sat beside her on the couch, turned her to face him and lifted her foot to his lap. He bent over, studying her foot. With the tweezers, he gently extracted the piece of glass lodged in her skin.

"Sorry," he said.

"For what?" she asked.

"If I hurt you."

"I've been hurt worse," she said. "It's just a little cut. Put a Band-Aid on it. I'll be all right."

He washed her foot, gently removing all the blood, and applied a square of gauze and some medical adhesive tape to hold the gauze in place. "When it stops bleeding, I'll put a regular bandage on it. For now, you need a little extra pressure to stem the flow of blood."

"Now who's the nurse?" she asked with a smile.

He looked up into her eyes. "I've done this a time or two."

Her smile faded. "As Delta Force, I can imagine you did."

"We're trained in self-aid buddy care. If one of our guys gets hurt, we gotta be ready to assist until the medical staff gets there. We do have a medic on the team, too. Sometimes he's not close enough to stop the bleeding quick enough. And when you're in a battle, you just have to patch and go as quickly as possible."

She touched his hand on her foot. "Sounds intense, like something nightmares are made of."

He nodded. "I've had a few nightmares. I can imagine you're having a few of your own." He turned his hand over and captured hers in his.

Deputy Jones entered through the front door, a German shepherd at her side. "We searched the area. Whoever it is, is long gone. My dog didn't even pick up his scent. He must have got into a vehicle and driven away. We lost his scent pretty abruptly."

Once again, her attacker had gotten away. Tessa should have shot him when she'd had the chance. "Thank you for checking," she said.

The sheriff came through the door behind her. "Ms. Bolton, are you all right?"

She nodded. "Irish is taking care of me."

The sheriff grinned. "Then you're in good hands."

She squeezed Irish's fingers. "Yes, sir. I am." But how long could she rely on him to protect her? She couldn't afford a bodyguard and the man had a job at the Whiskey Gulch Ranch.

The sheriff had questions. While he asked them, Irish left the couch and went into the kitchen.

The sound of broken glass being cleaned up reached Tessa in the living room. "You don't have to do that," she called out.

Irish responded, "Yes I do. My mother taught me better."

The sheriff shook his head. "Let the man clean. How often do you get a man to clean your kitchen?"

Tessa almost said *never.* But that was her ex-husband Randy. Irish was a completely different man. And right then she was glad that it was Irish who'd come to help her. She valued her independence, but there was a limit to how independent she could be when somebody was breaking into her house.

For it to take Irish only two minutes to get to her, he could not have gone out to Whiskey Gulch Ranch. He must have stayed somewhere close by. For that, she was grateful. She didn't know what she would have done had that intruder broken through her bedroom door. She'd never shot someone before, but she wouldn't hesitate to do it if her life depended on it.

Chapter Six

As Irish cleaned up the glass in the kitchen, his chest tightened. The blood on the floor was only a fraction of what it could have been had her attacker gotten to her. He swept the glass into a dustpan and dumped it into the trash receptacle. With a damp mop, he cleaned the blood off the floor. The sheriff warned Irish not to touch the back doorknob or anything around the door so that they could dust for prints.

The sound of Tessa's voice in the other room as she spoke with the sheriff and the deputy reassured him she was going to be all right. The glass on the back door of the kitchen would have to be replaced. Or, better still, Irish would recommend that instead of glass she replace the door with something more solid.

Irish thanked his lucky stars that he hadn't gone back to Whiskey Gulch Ranch like he'd told her he would. He'd made it all the way to the other side of town before he'd applied the brakes and turned around. Instead of heading out to the ranch, he'd pulled into the parking lot of the local watering hole,

Stew & Brew, figuring he could stay there until they closed somewhere around two in the morning.

Out at the ranch, he would have worried that cell phone reception was spotty. If Tessa had tried to get hold of him out there, the call might not have gone through until it was too late for him to help. The distance to the ranch would have been detrimental as well. It would have taken him more than fifteen minutes to get to her house. As it was, he'd just stepped out of the bar, debating whether or not to bed down in his truck and sleep the night away in the parking lot, when he'd received her call. He'd driven like a bat out of hell to get to her before the attacker did, all the while dialing 9-1-1 to get the sheriff's deputies out there as well.

Once he'd arrived, he found her front door locked. When Tessa had screamed, Irish had nearly lost his mind. His heart had leaped into his throat and he'd run for the back door. When he'd come through the open door of the house to find her standing barefoot in the kitchen with a gun pointed at his chest, he couldn't help the relief he'd felt. Sure, she could have put a bullet through him, but she was alive.

He made quick work of the kitchen cleanup. Once he was finished, he got a glass out of the cabinet, filled it with ice and water and carried it into the living room where Tessa was still talking with the sheriff and deputy.

"We've done all that we can do here," the sheriff was saying. "Do you want me to leave Deputy Jones positioned outside your house for the night?"

"That won' be necessary," Irish said. "I'll be positioned outside the house for the remainder of the night, and every night until her attacker is apprehended." He turned to Tessa. "Unless Ms. Bolton would prefer to have two people watching her house through the rest of the night, one should do."

Tessa's gaze met his. She turned to the sheriff. "Irish is right, having Deputy Jones here won't be necessary if Irish is staying. I won't need somebody else standing guard. Besides, I'm sure Deputy Jones has plenty of other areas that she needs to patrol tonight."

The sheriff nodded. "As you wish. We'll be back in the daylight to see if we can find any evidence that your intruder might have left behind."

"Thank you, Sheriff Barron. And thank you, Deputy Jones. I appreciate you coming out so quickly."

The sheriff shook his head. "I wish we had more to go on. One thing's for sure, you're definitely being targeted. This was his second attempt to get you."

Irish had had the same thought. The attack on River Road could have been an attack of convenience. But he was almost sure the break-in tonight had been committed by the same perp. It was personal. He wanted Tessa. No one else.

"I'm worried about you being out here all by yourself," the sheriff said.

Tessa shook her head. "I'll be fine."

Irish said, "I'll make sure she's protected."

"Then we'll be going," the sheriff said. "I'm glad

you're okay, Ms. Bolton." He and Deputy Jones left the house.

Irish stood at the door waiting for the sheriff and the deputy's vehicle lights to disappear down the end of the road. Then he turned to Tessa. "Do you have a sheet of plywood or something that I could use to cover the back window on the door in the kitchen?" he asked.

She shrugged. "The house came with a shed in the back. I'm not sure exactly what's out there other than the lawn mower. There might be some spare wood."

His lips twisted. "You wouldn't happen to have a hammer and some nails as well, would you?"

Again she shrugged. "I really don't know. I haven't had to do any repairs since I've been here, and I haven't been here that long. I bought this house from a retired couple who moved back to San Antonio to be closer to their daughter. I don't think Mr. Fellows took everything out of his shed when he and his wife moved out. You might find some tools and supplies in there. Let me get a flashlight." Tessa pushed to her feet and winced when her foot hit the floor.

Irish's lips pressed into a thin line. "You stay put. I'll take care of this."

She shook her head. "I have to get used to walking on that foot 'cause I have to work tomorrow."

Irish frowned. "Can't you call in sick?"

"No," Tessa said. "They're already shorthanded. I need to be there, even if I'm limping."

"Well, you don't have to be on your feet now. Just

sit there. I'll take care of this. And have your gun ready." He moved her handgun closer to her on the coffee table.

"I'm not sure where my flashlight is," Tessa said. "I think it's in one of the drawers in the kitchen. The one closest to the refrigerator."

Irish went to the kitchen and rummaged through the drawer next to the refrigerator, finding a small flashlight that would do little to help him locate any of the supplies he needed. Leaving the kitchen, he went back through the living room and out the front door.

"Where are you going?" Tessa asked.

"Out to get a real flashlight," he said.

He located his large flashlight behind the seat of his truck. He kept it there in case he broke down along the side of the road.

Flashlight in hand, he rounded the side of the house and hurried to where the shed sat in the far corner of the yard.

Inside the shed, Irish didn't find plywood, but he found a couple of boards and a container of nails. And he was lucky enough to locate a hammer in one of the drawers. He carried the boards, the nails and hammer back to the house and went to work covering the hole left on the back door, hammering away to accomplish the task. When he was done, he went inside, locked the door, and walked through to the living room area where Tessa sat on the couch.

"It's not pretty, but it will do for the night," he

said. "Tomorrow, I will go to the hardware store and look for a new door."

"Thank you," Tessa said. "I'd do it myself but I'm gonna be at work." She tipped her head to the side. "But won't that make you late for your job?"

Irish shook his head. "I spoke with Trace. He's all for me sticking with you until we figure out who's attacking you. I told you, he has a security business startup and this is right up his alley as far as what he had in mind for us to do."

Tessa frowned. "I don't have the kind of money it takes to hire a personal bodyguard," she said. "I barely have enough money to make the payments on this house and the utilities."

Irish held up his hands. "Don't worry about it. Trace inherited enough money to allow him to take all cases, whether they could pay or not."

Tessa drew in a breath and let it out. "I hate this."

Irish nodded. "I do, too."

"I went from feeling safe and secure in my own home, to not having a place I can go and feel safe."

"I get that," Irish said. "If it makes you feel any better, I'll be right outside in my truck. If you need me, all you have to do is yell. I'll hear you. Do you want help getting back to your bedroom?"

She shook her head and stood, trying not to put too much weight on her injured foot. "I think I'll be all right. If I just put my weight on the ball of my foot, I won't hit the spot where the glass cut my heel."

"In that case, follow me to the door, if you can,

and lock it behind me when I go out," he said. He started for the front entrance.

Tessa followed. "Are you sure you're going to stay all night in your truck?"

He chuckled. "Trust me. It's a lot more comfortable than a foxhole." He cupped her face. "I'm sorry this is happening to you. But I'll do my best to take care of you and make sure that nothing else happens again."

She leaned into the palm of his hand. "It's not your fault," she said. "You weren't the one who attacked me," Tessa said.

Still," he said, "no one deserves this."

"True. It shouldn't happen. But it does all too often," Tessa said. "Thank you for being here for me."

Irish brushed his lips across her forehead. "Don't forget to lock the door behind me," he said and stepped out onto the porch.

"Irish," she called out.

He turned. His gaze captured hers. "I'll only be a few steps away. All you have to do is call my name, yell, whistle—anything to get my attention."

She shook her head. "You can't sleep in your truck. You're a big guy. You'd be too uncomfortable."

"I'll be fine. Just being close will ease my mind." He turned again. "Don't forget to lock the door."

"Irish," she said with a sigh. "Come back inside. You can sleep on the couch."

He turned to face her. "I don't want to make you

uncomfortable. I'm only here to make sure that you're safe. The truck will be fine for me."

"I would feel more comfortable having you inside the house rather than out in your truck," Tessa said. "Please, come back inside."

Irish entered the house, closed the door and locked it. "If at any time you feel uncomfortable with me being inside the house with you, let me know. That truck is just fine with me."

Tessa smiled. "After all you've done for me? I'm not afraid of you, Irish. Everything you've done has been to help not, hurt me. Besides, I would feel really bad if you got a crick in your neck or threw your back out because you slept in your truck. The couch is surprisingly comfortable. I think you'll be all right on it. And I'll feel safer knowing you're just a few steps away." She limped into the hallway and came back out with a blanket and a pillow.

"Help yourself to anything in the kitchen. I have deli meat in the refrigerator and bread in the pantry. You can make a sandwich. I even have some leftover spaghetti, if you're hungry for more of a meal."

"Thanks," he said. "I had a hamburger at the bar. But if you feel like having a sandwich or some spaghetti, I'd be happy to fix it for you."

She shook her head. "No, I'm ready to get some sleep. I have an early morning and its almost that time now. Thanks for being here. Good night."

"Good night, Tessa," Irish said.

Tessa limped into her bedroom and closed the

door behind her. A moment later, she cracked it open just a bit.

Irish stretched out on the couch and leaned back against the pillow. He could see Tessa's door from where he lay and took comfort knowing that nobody would get past him to her without him putting up a fight first. He linked his hands behind his neck and closed his eyes.

Sleep didn't come until the wee hours of the morning, and he was up again at sunrise. Until they caught the attacker, he would be with Tessa every minute of the day except for when she was at the hospital working. Even then, he considered asking the hospital staff if he could follow her around to make sure she wouldn't be ambushed in some dark corner.

He suspected Tessa would be resistant to him intruding on her work. *Baby steps,* he told himself. He'd take baby steps to make sure that she would be all right.

Irish had coffee ready and scrambled eggs cooking in a small skillet when Tessa limped into the kitchen dressed in scrubs. He hoped that this day would be a lot better for her than the day before.

"Good morning, sunshine," he said.

She inhaled deeply, closing her eyes. "Is that coffee I smell?"

He nodded. "Sure is. Wanna cup?"

"I'd love a cup." She pinched the bridge of her nose. "I feel like my eyelids are sandpaper today."

"That's understandable," he said. "You maybe got three hours of sleep last night."

"I'm sure you didn't get much more than that," she said.

"I got enough." He poured coffee into a mug and handed it to her. "I'm sure you know where the sugar and milk are, if you need it."

"Black's good for me," she said. "Anything to wake me up. It's gonna be a long day at the hospital."

Irish scraped the scrambled eggs out of the pan onto a plate. "I wish you'd really consider calling in sick. That foot's going to make it a miserable day for you."

She sighed. "I can't. I'm too new at this job. I have to be there. Besides, I can put a little bit of weight on it today. It's tender, but I can do this."

"You are one determined lady," Irish said.

"I have to be to make it in this world," she said. "There's no such thing as a free ride."

He laid the plate of scrambled eggs on the table. "Have a seat. Your eggs are ready." The toast popped up and he removed the two slices. He laid once piece on her plate and one on the plate he had for himself on the counter. He went back to work cracking eggs into the pan.

Tessa sat at the table. "So, you're good with animals. You're good with a gun. And now you're proving to be good in the kitchen. What else should I know about you, Irish?"

"My mom and dad both had full-time jobs when I was growing up, and I'm the oldest and have two younger sisters I had to take care of. Getting them ready to go to school, getting them off the bus and watching them after school was my job. I'm handy in the kitchen out of necessity. I can braid hair, and I make a good guest at a tea party." He gave her a side-eyed glance. "I trust you won't tell the guys. I'd never hear the end of it."

She grinned and held up her hand as if swearing in court. "Your secret is safe with me."

"Glad to hear it." He scraped eggs onto his plate, carried the plate over to the table and sat down across from her.

"I'm surprised some woman hasn't snapped you up. With those qualifications, you're a great catch." Tessa took a bite out of her eggs and looked over her plate at him.

Irish shook his head. "The timing was never right. As long as I was with Delta Force, the army owned me. My first allegiance was to the military. Any relationship with a woman would have taken second place. It wouldn't have been fair." He looked across the table at her. "But you were married. No children?"

She pushed her eggs around the plate with her fork. "I wanted children," she said. "My ex didn't. The world seemed to revolve around him. He couldn't have handled the competition a child would bring into a relationship." She lifted one shoulder. "It's just as well. When he started hitting me, I knew that would be no way to raise a child. I'm really glad we didn't have children."

"Have you given up on the idea of children?" Irish asked.

Tessa's gaze shifted to the window. "I don't know. I'm not anxious to get back into a relationship. Apparently, I have bad taste in men. Who's to say I wouldn't choose unwisely again? And I couldn't bring a child into a world where his father is an abuser."

Irish reached across the table and took her hand. "Not all men are like your ex-husband," he said. "And you were young when you married him. You couldn't have known that he was an abuser until he actually started hitting you."

"I should have known," Tessa said. "He was always very self-centered. He got a big head from being the captain of the football team and homecoming king. He could do no wrong. I was a cheerleader. He was a quarterback. It was a foregone conclusion that we would marry, even though we went our separate ways in college. We knew we'd end up married when we graduated. And we did."

Irish squeezed her hand. "What happened?"

She stared down at where their hands were linked. "I think the stress of his job made him angry. And he took that anger out on the only person he had available. Me. I know all men aren't the same. But having survived a bad relationship, I'm not eager to get into another anytime soon." Tessa released his hand, finished her eggs and carried her plate to the sink, limping all the way. "I'll be at the hospital all day, so I won't need you to protect me. I'll have people all around me and I promise not to leave the hospital until I get off work."

"Are you sure you'll be all right by yourself? Even in the hospital?" he asked.

"I'm usually very busy, and rarely alone. There are always people around me." She smiled. "Besides, I'm sure the horses miss you and want you to be there to feed them."

"I have backup at Whiskey Gulch Ranch. They're not completely reliant on me to take care of the animals."

Tessa held up a hand. "I promise I'll be okay. You can spend the day out there."

He finished his breakfast and carried his plate to the sink, rinsing it and putting it in the dishwasher along with hers. "I would like to take care of that back door for you. But I can do that after I take care of the animals out at the ranch."

She smiled. "Good. I didn't want to disrupt your day any more than I have to."

He took her hands in his. "You are not disrupting my day. When I'm not with you, I'm worried about you. I'll be there when you get off work. You get off at the same time every day, don't you?"

She nodded. "I do. As long as there's not anything major going on in the hospital. Sometimes I have to pull a second shift. I'll let you know with a phone call or text message if that happens."

"Fair enough. I'll be there when you come out of the hospital to ensure you make it safely to your car and then to your home."

She smiled. "Thanks. All I have to do now is brush my teeth and I'll be ready to go. I have an extra toothbrush in the guest bathroom if you care to use it."

"Thanks, and when I'm out at the ranch, I'll be sure to grab my shaving kit. Until they catch that guy, I prefer to stay here with you. I hope you don't mind."

She shook her head. "After last night? No, not at all. I'm glad you're here."

"Good. I thought I was going to have to fight you again today."

She grinned. "Not today."

They went to their separate bathrooms. Irish found the spare toothbrush package and a small tube of toothpaste. He brushed his teeth and washed his face. Afterward, he rubbed his hand across the roughness of his beard and studied his reflection in the mirror. It would have to do for now. When he got out to the ranch, he'd grab what he needed and bring it back with him. In the meantime, he had to get Tessa to work on time.

She came out of her bedroom slinging her purse over her shoulder. "Ready?"

He nodded. "You could ride with me, you know. If I'm following you home from work, it just doesn't make sense that we ride in separate vehicles."

She shook her head. "If it's all the same to you, I'd prefer to drive my own car. Just in case something comes up and you don't get there on time."

He gave her a stern look. "I'm serious about not leaving the hospital without me there."

She drew in a deep breath. "I really like having my own vehicle."

"Fair enough. I'll follow you. You lead the way."

With her key in hand, she stepped through the door and waited for him to come out and close it behind him. She locked the door behind both of them and handed him the key. "You'll need that to work on the back door."

Irish pocketed the key and followed her out to her SUV. He checked the back seat before she got in. Once he was sure that there was nobody in it, she got in, cranked her vehicle, and he got in his truck and followed her to the hospital. Once there, he escorted her inside like the he'd done the day before.

She turned and waved. "I can handle it from here."

He stepped back, letting the sliding glass doors close. He didn't like leaving her, even for a moment. But she was right. There were a lot of people around her in the hospital. And she wouldn't be alone at any time during the day.

Irish went back to his truck and sat there for a few moments watching the vehicles in the parking lot. The people going in and out. Suspicious of everyone. No one looked like a murderer as far as he could tell. When he could sit there no longer, he started the engine. He had work to do, so he headed out to the ranch, hoping that Tessa would be okay that day. When he came back into town, he would stop at the sheriff's office and see if they'd made any headway on finding out who had attacked Tessa.

Chapter Seven

Tessa entered the ER that morning like any other day, except that she was limping. And she'd barely slept because she'd had an intruder in her house. Yeah, it wasn't like every other day. She made it past the admissions desk and into the restricted area before being accosted by her coworker.

Allison was emerging from an examination room when she spotted her. "Tessa! Girl. That's it. You *have* to come stay with me."

Tessa grimaced. "I take it you've heard."

"Heard? Hell!" she exclaimed. "Everyone in the hospital has heard." Allison frowned. "And you're limping. What the hell? He hurt you, didn't he?"

Tessa shook her head. "Not actually. I was chasing him out the back door when I stepped on the glass from the broken window in my kitchen."

Allison winced. "Ouch. Come here, let's have a look at that foot." She led Tessa into an empty exam room and made her sit on the bed.

"I'm really okay," Tessa said. "We cleaned the

wound, applied some antibiotic ointment and put a pressure dressing on it. It should be okay."

"I'll be the judge of that," Allison said and removed Tessa's shoe and sock. "Nice dressing," she said. "The EMT do this?"

"No." Heat rushed up Tessa's neck into her cheeks. "Irish did."

Allison glanced up from Tessa's foot. Her eyebrows rising.

Tessa groaned. "Now don't go reading anything into that. He was the first on the scene. I called him as soon as the intruder broke the glass in my kitchen door."

Allison smirked. "So you called Irish first instead of 9-1-1?"

"It was the last number keyed into my phone. What can I say? It was easiest just to hit Redial."

Allison nodded with a quirky lift to the corner of one side of her mouth. "Uh-huh. You sure it wasn't that he was staying the night there?"

Tessa shook her head. "Contrary to what you might think, I'm not ready for that kind of a relationship."

Allison sighed. "You really do need to get out and date. Not all men are like your ex."

"I know," Tessa said. "And Irish is nothing like Randy. It's just that I'm trying to get used to liking myself. I need to learn to trust my own judgment again. I thought Randy was perfect for me, until I married him."

"High school relationships aren't always an indicator of a lifetime relationship," Allison said.

Tessa snorted. "Like you're an example? You and Brian have been together for how long now?"

Allison grinned. "Since eighth grade. But he's the exception to the rule," she said. "He's always been and always will be a gentleman. He never forgets my birthday and never forgets Valentine's Day. He never forgets the first day we kissed. Even when he was deployed for fourteen months, he managed to get a box of chocolates and flowers to me for Valentine's Day. He'd arranged with one of the florists in the town where we were stationed to have them delivered so I wouldn't miss out."

"Now why couldn't Randy have been like that? Although, gifts aren't what count. What really mattered was that he never displayed any of the little things that indicated true love."

Allison gave a gentle smile. "Like reaching for your hand for no reason at all?"

Tessa nodded.

Allison sighed and pressed her hands to her chest. "Or opening the door for you when your hands are full of groceries?" She grinned. "Or insisting that that he bring in all the groceries since you did all the shopping."

"No," Tessa said. "He doesn't have to. A good man shows his love in everything he does for his woman."

Allison gave Tessa a secret little smile. "Like sticking around town when he doesn't have to? Or being there as soon as he can when your house is broken in to? And dressing your wound like a professional?"

Tessa rolled her eyes. "And we're back to Irish, I take it?"

Allison nodded. "He is rather a hunk."

Tessa couldn't deny that. The man had broad shoulders, thickly muscled arms, a narrow waist and hips, and tight thighs. She would never forget the sculptured thighs. She'd admired him on more than one occasion. Tessa shook her head. "He was just being nice, and now I understand that he has also been assigned to me by his friend Trace Travis to be my personal bodyguard."

Allison's eyebrows shot up. "Seriously?"

Tessa nodded. "Trace Travis is setting up some kind of security firm and hiring some of his military buddies to man it."

Allison removed the bandage on Tessa's foot. "And here I thought Irish was a simple ranch hand."

Tessa chuckled. "Irish is anything but simple. You know the man was Delta Force, right?"

"I had heard that he was prior military," Allison said. "But Delta Force? Wow. Those guys are the best of the best, aren't they?" Allison looked down at the bandage she had pulled away. "I guess that explains why he is so good at dressing a wound. Those guys have to be able to do that kind of thing out in the field." Allison glanced around. "So, if he's your bodyguard, where is he?"

"I told him I didn't need him while I was at the

hospital. I have plenty of people around me to keep me safe."

"I hope you're right," Allison cautioned. "Just make sure that you're around folks all of the time. No darting into janitor's closets or dark rooms by yourself."

"I'll be all right. The people at the front desk don't let just anybody back here in the restricted area," Tessa said.

Allison shook her head. "True. However, someone who has the nerve to break into your house to attack you might consider that a challenge he can't resist."

Tessa's mouth formed a thin line. "Trust me. Now that I know he is specifically after me, I will remain ultra-aware of everything around me."

Allison studied Tessa's heel. "Looks like your wound is going to be all right. There's no swelling or redness." She swiped alcohol across it, let it dry and then applied a fresh bandage. One that wasn't quite as thick, since it had quit bleeding. "I'd advise you to stay off your feet, but since you're here at work, that's not a possibility. At least limit the number of hours that you're standing on the injured area, if you can."

"I'll do my best," Tessa said. "Thanks."

She went to work, balancing on the ball of her foot when treating patients and entering data into the computer system. Though her lunch break was short, she managed to put her throbbing foot up. During her shift, she had little relief from being on her feet. That was okay by Tessa. Sitting still during the lulls between patients gave her too much time to think about the attack. And about Irish. An unwelcome thrill of excitement fluttered through her the closer she came to the end of the day. Irish would be staying at her house again tonight. Sleeping on her couch. She'd see him when she got off work because he'd be there in the parking lot waiting for her.

Thirty minutes before the end of her shift, her relief nurse called in to say that she would be late by at least two hours. Could someone fill in for her?

"I can do it," Allison said. "No, wait. I have to be at my apartment immediately after work for the service technician to fix my air conditioner." She pressed her lips together. "I'd call and reschedule, but this was the company's first available appointment."

Tessa shook her head. "It's okay. I can stay."

Allison frowned. "You've been limping through this day like a trooper. I'll just call and have the maintenance guy come another day."

Tessa held up her hands. "It's okay. Things are getting kind of slow. I can sit down a few times and put my foot up. Sleeping at night without an air conditioner in this heat is insane. You need to go."

"I would have Brian do it, but he doesn't get off duty until seven tomorrow morning."

"I've got this," Tessa said. "You go take care of your AC."

Allison left at five o'clock.

Tessa texted Irish and told him she wouldn't be off until seven and not to come any earlier. He replied, "Okay."

As soon as Allison left, an ambulance rolled in with a teenager who'd been in a motorcycle accident. Tessa and the on-call doctor worked to stabilize him and then prepared him for transport to a bigger hospital in San Antonio more equipped to work with head injuries. By the time they had him loaded into the ambulance for transport, an elderly man entered the ER suffering with chest pains. He was followed by a child with a ruptured eardrum, a cowboy who'd stepped on a nail, a snake bite victim, and a case of pneumonia.

Tessa felt a hand on her shoulder. The nurse who had called in had arrived. It had only been an hour and a half of the two hours she had said she would be.

"Sorry I was late," she said. "I'll take over from here. You go home. Get some rest."

Tessa nodded. Her foot throbbed, a headache was forming behind her eyes, and she was exhausted. After thirteen and a half hours on her feet, she was ready to jump in the shower and hit the bed. Grabbing her purse from the locker room, she left the hospital and trudged out to her SUV in the parking lot. Clouds had moved in, making it dark even sooner than normal. She hadn't realized that she hadn't parked under a light. Before she reached her vehicle, she stopped, remembering she'd told Irish she'd wait for him.

A noise behind her made her look back. A large, shadowy figure ran toward her. Tessa's heart leaped as she couldn't make out the face of the person heading straight for her. Gut instinct told her to run.

Headlights flashed in the parking lot and an engine revved. Caught between the man rushing at her and headlights now racing toward her, Tessa screamed. The man grabbed her arm, jerked her backward and wrapped his arms around her waist, trapping her against his chest. Then he dragged her behind a car.

The vehicle speeding through the parking lot made a sharp turn, its tires squealing against the pavement.

Tessa fought to break free of the man who held her tightly against his body.

"Let me go!" she yelled.

The vehicle spun in a circle and headed back toward Tessa and her captor. When it was clear that the vehicle was coming straight for her, Tessa worked with the man holding her around the middle to get out of the way of the oncoming car. Before she could guess his intentions, her captor threw her over the hood of the car they were standing beside and slid across after her.

The vehicle charging toward them smashed into the side of the car where they had been standing moments before, pushing the vehicle toward where Tessa had landed on the ground.

A hand grabbed hers. She was yanked to her feet and dragged away from the car that was sliding sideways.

"Run, Tessa!" a familiar voice shouted. "Run!"

A sob rose up Tessa's throat. The man who had grabbed her was Irish. The attacking vehicle backed away from the one it had crushed, drove around it and started toward Irish and Tessa. Irish pulled his handgun from a holster beneath his jacket and pointed it at the driver.

"Run, Tessa," he said.

Tessa couldn't make her feet move. She stood, gripped in horror at what was happening.

Irish would be crushed beneath the wheels of the vehicle barreling at him.

Irish fired a shot. The vehicle swerved and raced out of the parking lot onto the street, tires screeching against pavement once again.

Tessa ran to Irish, threw her arms around his waist and clung to him. "I thought he would run you over," she said, a sob choking her words.

"I would have moved out of the way in time," he said, smoothing a hand over her hair.

"He was coming at you so fast, I didn't think you would get away."

He chuckled. "So, does that mean you care?"

"Yes, I care." Tessa buried her face against his shirt and murmured, "Who else would be my bodyguard?"

"Why did you run from me?" he asked.

She shook her head. "I didn't know it was you. I thought it was somebody trying to abduct me. I did the only thing I could and ran. Then the car and... and...you threw me over the other car."

"I did. I had to get you out of the driver's path." He set her at arm's length. "Were you hurt?"

She shook her head. "I'm okay. Maybe a little

bruised, but that's better than crushed between the grill of that lunatic's vehicle and the car he hit."

Irish's jaw tightened. "Exactly. I figured throwing you over the hood would do less damage." He took her hand. "Come on. Let's get you home. You can ride with me this time. We don't know where that guy went or if he's waiting to run into your car next."

Tessa didn't argue. She let Irish lead her toward his truck in the dark.

As they walked, Irish pulled his cell phone from his pocket and dialed 9-1-1. He gave a description of the vehicle and explained the incident. "I'd give you a license plate, but it had been removed," Irish said.

Tessa had been more worried about surviving either a man's attack or being crushed be two tons of metal. She hadn't even had the time to get a description of the vehicle, much less a license plate number. She was impressed by Irish's ability to observe in a time of stress.

Irish opened the door to his truck for Tessa to climb in. When she stumbled on the step, he gripped her around the waist and lifted her up and into the seat. His hands remained on her waist for a long moment as he stared up into her eyes. "Why didn't you wait for me to get here?"

She sighed. "I know I should have. But it was such a busy day, and I was so tired when I got off work, I didn't think. I was in go-home mode."

Irish chuckled. "Like a horse headed for the barn."

She laughed. "You're comparing me to a horse?"

He grinned. "I have the highest respect for horses."

"I guess that's okay then," she said.

"Buckle up, sweetheart." He closed the door, rounded the front of the truck and slid into the driver's seat. "Maybe I should stay with you all day while you're at work."

"I might consider it, if this situation goes on much longer," Tessa said. "But not tomorrow."

"Why not tomorrow?" Irish asked.

She smiled and leaned her head back against the headrest. "I'm off for the next three days."

"Good," Irish said. "I'll spend the next three days strictly with you."

Tessa frowned. "You have to have better things to do than follow around behind me like a babysitter."

He shook his head. "Nope. Trace has me covered. This is my assignment. *You* are officially my assignment."

Her eyes still closed, she sighed. "That sounds so impersonal. Which is just as well."

"Why do you say that?" Irish asked.

She leaned her head to the side and opened her eyes to look at him. "As cute as you are in your jogging shorts, I don't need to get into another relationship."

Irish grinned. "So, you think I'm cute in my jogging shorts?"

Heat climbed up Tessa's neck into her cheeks. Why did she have to say that? "I must be really tired to have said that. But, yes, you do have a really nice physique. I'd be blind if I didn't notice. But don't think that that means anything."

He drove toward her house with a grin on his face.

Tessa couldn't help but smile herself. After the past two days, his cheerfulness made a difference in her life. She really needed to smile and laugh more. "I'm not sure what I have in my refrigerator, but you are welcome to stay and have dinner with me."

He shook his head. "I took the liberty of stocking your refrigerator, since I'll be staying with you for an unknown amount of time. And while I did that, I took care of that back door and replaced it with a solid one."

Tessa sat up straight and turned toward him. "You got all that done in just one day?"

He shrugged. "I can be pretty handy when I want to be. The door needs a coat of paint, but we can do that tomorrow while we're there."

"Why are you doing this for me?" she asked. "Surely that can't be part of the job of a bodyguard?"

"Gotta take care of my jogging buddy," he said. "You're the high point of my day when I jog the river trail."

Tessa didn't say it out loud, but Irish was the high point of her day as well. She always looked forward to seeing him run toward her and say hello.

"How do grilled steaks and baked potatoes sound for dinner tonight?" Irish asked.

Tessa snorted. "That would sound wonderful, if I had a grill."

"Then how does broiled steaks and baked potatoes sound?" Irish shot a glance her way.

"Perfect." She grinned. "I take it you're doing the cooking?" she asked.

He nodded. "I am. Have to keep the little woman off her feet. Speaking of which, how is your foot today?"

It throbbed now that she had the weight off it, like it was getting more blood to the injured area. "Achy, but I'll survive."

He pulled into her driveway, parked the truck and came around to her side to open the door. When she started to get out of the truck, he scooped her up and carried her to the front steps.

She wrapped her arm around his shoulders and held on until he reached the top of the steps. "My foot might ache a little, but I'm perfectly capable of walking on it," she said.

"I know." He winked and set her down long enough to unlock the front door. "Stay here. I'll be right back."

Tessa leaned against the wall and waited, her breath lodged in her throat, her pulse pounding.

A minute later, he was back. "All clear."

She let go of the breath she'd been holding. "How do people live like this?"

"Like what?" he asked.

She shook her head. "In fear of walking into their own home?"

"We'll catch that guy. He's got to slip up soon. Hopefully they'll locate the vehicle that he used as a battering ram and trace him through that."

"Unless he stole it," Tessa suggested.

"If he was smart, that's what he did," Irish said.

He led her into the house, turned, closed and locked the door behind them. "The question is, what did you do to piss him off?"

"I only wish I knew," Tessa said. As she set her purse on the counter, her cell phone rang. She glanced down at the caller ID and frowned. "Why is he calling?" she asked aloud.

"He who?" Irish asked.

"My ex-husband." She stared at the phone without picking it up. "Question is, should I answer it?"

"You say that you don't think that it was him who attacked you, but what if it was? Or what if he had hired somebody to do the job?"

Tessa shook her head. "Why would he do that? I gave him everything in the divorce—the house, the car, the bank account…everything but my clothes. All I wanted was away from him."

"Who initiated the divorce?" Irish asked.

Tessa's lips formed a thin line. "I did."

Irish shrugged. "Some men don't take rejection very well."

The phone rang again.

"Maybe you should answer it," Irish said. "Maybe he's calling to confess."

Tessa's jaw hardened as she pressed the button to answer the call.

"Tessa." Randy's voice came over the line, making her belly knot.

"What do you want, Randy?" Tessa asked tersely.

"I'll be in Whiskey Gulch tomorrow night and would like to meet with you, if I could?"

"Tomorrow night?" Tessa challenged. "Or are you already in Whiskey Gulch?"

"I don't know what you mean." He sounded confused. But then Randy was good at acting. He'd pretended to love her for all the years they were married. "No, I'm in San Antonio, but I'm headed to Whiskey Gulch tomorrow night and I'd like to meet with you. Would you consider having dinner with me?"

Her first inclination was to say no. But if he was responsible for the attacks, meeting with him might help to get a confession out of him. "Okay," she said. "I'll meet you for dinner tomorrow night, but somewhere public."

"That would be fine," Randy said. "Name the place."

"The diner on Main Street at six o'clock." Tessa's gaze met Irish's.

"I'll be there," Randy said.

Tessa ended the call without saying goodbye.

"Sounds like you have a date with your ex-husband," Irish said.

She nodded. "I wouldn't call it a date. I agreed to meet with him. And if he's the one who's causing all these attacks..." Her lips pursed. "I'll take him down."

Irish reached out to take her hand. "And I'll be with you tomorrow night when you have that meeting with him."

Tessa frowned. "He might not confess if you're sitting with me. He's really good at bullying women when he's alone with them—or with me. When he's with other men, it's like he's a completely different person."

"I admit, I don't like the idea of you being anywhere close to him," Irish said.

"Me, either," Tessa said. "It took a lot for me to get away from him to begin with."

"Then call him back and cancel. You shouldn't have to deal with him," Irish said.

"I'm not the same person I was when I was married to him." Tessa lifted her chin. "I won't let him bully me anymore." She gave him a quick smile. "But if you could be somewhere nearby, that would make me feel a little better about being in the same building with him."

"Deal," Irish said. "I'll be in the booth next to yours. If he even hints at raising a hand to you, I'll be there to stop him."

"Okay, then—" Tessa squeezed his hand "—I'll meet with him."

She wasn't looking forward to meeting with Randy. He hadn't taken their divorce very well. But if he had anything to do with the attacks, she would find out. And meeting with him might be the only way.

Chapter Eight

Irish wasn't happy about the proposed dinner Tessa had planned with her ex-husband. If there was another way to get him to Whiskey Gulch for questioning, he'd do it in a heartbeat. Having him in town would give the sheriff's department a chance to interrogate him.

He lifted his cell to make the call to the sheriff when his phone rang. He glanced at the caller ID.

It was Trace Travis.

"Hey, boss," Irish answered.

"I'm at the sheriff's office right now with Deputy Jones. Do you mind if we come by and speak with Ms. Bolton?"

He glanced across at Tessa. "I don't mind, but let me check with her."

"I called you because I wanted to make sure she was up to it," Trace said. "I heard she was attacked again out in the parking lot of the hospital."

"If you have any news whatsoever about who the attacker might be, I'm sure she would love to hear."

He lifted his chin toward Tessa. "Are you up to a visit from Trace and Deputy Jones?"

She stepped toward him, nodding. "Like you just said, if it has anything to do with my attacker, I'm more than ready. Bring him on."

"How soon can you be here?" Irish asked.

"Give us five minutes," Trace said.

Irish ended the call. "Are you sure you're up to company?"

"Absolutely, as long as it has something to do with solving this case. I've racked my brain trying to figure out who could be mad enough to want to hurt me. Other than my ex-husband, I can't come up with a single clue."

"It's just as well then that your ex-husband is coming to town tomorrow…if he hasn't been here all along. None of your patients come to mind?" Irish asked. "You haven't recommended anyone for the psych ward?"

She shook her head. "Not one."

"Any old boyfriends coming out of the woodwork?" Irish tilted his head to one side. "I mean, you did move back from San Antonio. And this is your hometown. You're attractive and bound to be popular."

She smiled. "No, I dated my ex all throughout high school. He was the only person I dated." Her smile faded. "Everybody knew I was Randy's girl."

"Has anybody asked you out while you've been here?" He persisted. "Somebody you might have turned down?"

She shook her head. "I've pretty much kept to myself. I didn't want anybody to ask me out."

"You say your ex-husband was really angry when you hit him up with the divorce papers."

Tessa nodded.

Irish hesitated before asking, "Angry enough to want to kill you?"

She shrugged. "I don't know. Maybe." Her face was pale and she had dark circles beneath her eyes.

Irish cupped her cheek, his voice softening. "Do you want to get a shower while I make dinner?"

She leaned into his palm. "You're supposed to be my bodyguard. Not my personal chef and housekeeper."

"I've already had my shower and, as pretty as you are in scrubs, I'm sure you're covered in all kinds of hospital germs." He winked.

She nodded. "I do like to get out of my scrubs and take a shower as soon as I get home."

"Then go." He tuned her and gave her a gentle shove. "I'll hold off the sheriff's deputy and Trace until you get out."

"Thanks." Tessa entered her bedroom and closed the door.

With just a few minutes to spare, Irish hurried to the kitchen, pulled the steaks, which he'd had marinating for several hours, from the refrigerator, put them on a broiler pan. He then removed the potatoes from the pantry and scrubbed them. He didn't have time to bake the potatoes in the oven with the steak, so he poked holes in them and stuck them in the microwave for six minutes. He wouldn't start the steaks until after Trace and Deputy Jones's visit.

With everything ready, he left the kitchen and returned to the living room just in time to hear a knock at the door. As he walked across the living room floor, he could hear the water in the shower turning off. He opened the door to find Trace and Deputy Jones standing there. "Come in," he said, standing back. "Tessa's just finishing up in the shower. She'll be out in a moment."

"Good." Deputy Jones entered. "We have news."

"Good news, I hope," Irish said.

"I don't know about good news," Trace said. "But it's news."

Once they were inside, Irish closed the door. "Can I get you some coffee?"

"I'll pass," Trace said.

"I'd love some," Deputy Jones said. "I've got the night shift tonight, and I've been up most of the day searching through databases."

"It's gonna be a long night for you," Irish said.

"Did you get the door hung?" Trace asked.

Irish nodded. "Come see."

Trace, Irish and Deputy Jones entered the kitchen.

While Irish poured a cup of coffee for the deputy, Trace inspected the door. "Looks good. I'll bet Ms. Bolton will be glad that it's solid versus the one with the window in it. That makes it way too easy for a burglar to break in. All they have to do is reach through the broken window and turn the knob."

"That's exactly what he did. Thank goodness

Tessa heard him break the glass and had the fore-sight to have her gun close by. I still need to patch the bullet hole she blew through the door to her bed-room." He handed the cup of coffee to Deputy Jones. "Milk or sugar?"

"I'll take a little sugar," she said, and set the mug on the counter.

Irish handed her a bowl and spoon. Deputy Jones scooped sugar into her mug and stirred.

"I hope you have good news for me," Tessa said as she entered the kitchen. She wore gray athletic pants and a loose T-shirt. Her hair was still wet and was combed straight back from her forehead. On her feet she wore slippers and limped, favoring her injured heel.

Irish's jaw tightened. "The sooner they find the bastard, the better."

"I don't know about good news," Deputy Jones said. "Mr. Travis and I have been combing through databases this afternoon, searching for similar crimes against women."

"I didn't think there was a whole lot of crime here in this area," Tessa said.

"Normally there's not. Here, lately, we've had a few incidences of human trafficking," the deputy said, casting a glance at Trace. "Mr. Travis and Matt Hennessey have helped in solving some of those cases, which we have been really grateful for."

"That's pretty scary," Tessa said. "Human traf-ficking, here in Whiskey Gulch?"

"That's right," Deputy Jones conceded, her face set in grim lines.

"Do you think whoever attacked me is after me to sell me into some sex trade or something?" Tessa asked.

Irish's hands clenched into fists. "If that were the case, why then did he try to run you over in the parking lot of the hospital? Seems to me he wouldn't want to damage the goods."

"You're right," Deputy Jones said. "That wouldn't make sense. But then, this may not be a case of human trafficking."

"Then what do you think it is?" Tessa asked.

"I wasn't finding a whole lot of crimes against women in this area, so I expanded my search through all of Texas. The search was too broad. So I limited it to female victims in South Central Texas. Again, the search was too broad. I played with different parameters, including hair color of the victims, age, and even tried the occupation of nurse." Deputy Jones tipped her head toward Trace. "Mr. Travis picked it up from there."

"I went at it from a little different angle. In many cases, the victim usually knows his or her attacker. If this guy had murdered, raped or accosted anybody else, it might have been somebody in or from this town. So I searched through the records from the sheriff's office, looking for similar cases. Only one in this county stood out to me. She was born the same year as you were and died on her high school graduation night."

"Penny." Tessa's face turned white. "You're talking about Penny Stevens. She was murdered on graduation night."

Trace nodded. "That's right. Penny Stevens, age eighteen."

Irish went to stand beside Tessa and slipped his arm around her waist.

"That was thirteen years ago. What could that have to do with what's happening to me now?"

"On a hunch," Trace said, "I searched a list of your classmates. She wasn't the only one who has died."

Tessa gasped. "Who else?" she asked.

Deputy Jones jumped in. "Between the yearbook and the obituaries for the town, Mr. Travis and I searched the crime databases looking for more of your classmates."

"And we found them," Trace said. "Five years ago, Kitty Kitterman disappeared out of her home in Kerrville. They found her body three days later in a ditch off Interstate 30, fifty miles west of Kerrville."

Deputy Jones added, "Three years ago, Bethany York, who'd become a teacher in San Antonio, went missing from her home one night. They found her body a month later in a ditch beside Interstate 30, within five miles of where they'd found the Kitterman woman's body."

Tessa pressed a hand to her mouth. "Were those the only others from my class?"

"Yes," Jones said. "And now the attack on you."

"Did these three women and you have something

in common besides coming from the same high school graduation class?" Trace asked.

Tears sprang into Tessa's eyes. "Yes. We were all cheerleaders. The four of us were the seniors on the squad the year we graduated."

Jones's gaze shot to Trace. "Wow. We should have seen that. I guess we can now go through the list of the other classmates to figure out who had it in for the cheerleaders."

"Given the fact the victims were all in the same class and were cheerleaders, we have to believe that whoever murdered them knew them." Jones pinned Tessa with her gaze. "And he knows you."

Trace's brow furrowed. "And you'll know him."

Tessa leaned against Irish.

He tightened his hold around her waist.

She shook her head. "But who? Ours wasn't a large school. Which one of my classmates would want to kill us?"

Deputy Jones sighed. "We haven't nailed that down yet. We hoped you might have insight into your classmates."

Trace paced across the floor of the kitchen and turned to face Tessa. "Can you recall any incidents that may have happened in high school between the cheerleaders of the senior class and any of the guys in that class or any of the classes below?"

"I can't remember anything that would have caused someone to be so upset that they would murder the cheerleaders. I was too busy cheering at football games and organizing fundraisers. We all were."

Deputy Jones's lips twisted and she tapped her chin. "Was there a bad breakup between a cheerleader and one of the guys in your school?"

Tessa shook her head. "Not me. I was dating the quarterback from ninth grade on. Everybody knew I was Randy's girl."

Irish shifted next to her, retaining his hold around her waist. "What about the other cheerleaders?"

"They bounced around between different boyfriends. It could have happened." Tessa shook her head. "It's not like I can ask them now. They're dead." Tears streamed down her face. "Why did I not know this?"

"Kitty Kitterman had married a guy named Pearson," Trace said. "I talked with my mother. She and Kitty's mother were friends. She said the Kittermans left Whiskey Gulch after Kitty graduated high school. The York family had the same situation. They moved to Boerne, just outside San Antonio, after Bethany graduated. Penny Stevens's notice was the only that showed up in the Whiskey Gulch obituaries because she was the only one who still lived here."

"I can't believe we lost touch," Tessa whispered. "I should have been a better friend."

"People lose touch after high school." Irish pulled a chair out at the kitchen table and pressed her into it. He hated seeing Tessa so sad. Her tears ripped at his heart. He wanted to make her world right again.

"They were my friends," Tessa said. "My teammates."

"And you were busy surviving an abusive relationship with your husband. You can't beat yourself up about it," Irish said.

"Your husband was one of your classmates?" Deputy Jones asked.

Tessa nodded. "He was the quarterback of the football team. I was the head cheerleader."

"What were you saying about an abusive relationship?" Trace asked.

Tessa buried her face in her hands. "I divorced him after he'd beat me once too often."

Irish laid a hand on Tessa's shoulder, the anger he felt for Tessa's ex-husband burning like a blowtorch in his chest.

"Could he have been the one who attacked you?" Deputy Jones asked.

Tessa shook her head. "I didn't think so. I swear the guy who attacked me was bigger than my ex-husband. But then I haven't seen my ex in six months."

"She is, however, seeing him tomorrow night," Irish noted.

Tessa wiped the tears from her cheeks and looked up. "I am. We're meeting at the diner at six o'clock."

"I'll be there with her," Irish said.

"We can have a patrol car stationed close by. We can also have a plainclothes officer inside the diner," Deputy Jones said.

Trace gave Irish a chin lift. "Matt Hennessey and I can be there as well."

Tessa laughed, the sound catching on a sob. "I don't suppose you can position a metal detector at the door as well?"

Deputy Jones gave her half a smile. "I could ask the high school principal to borrow theirs for the evening."

Tessa glanced at the new back door. "Wow, this is all crazy." She shrugged. "But if Randy's the one doing this, we have to catch him. And we have to stop him from killing anybody else."

"Were there only four seniors on the cheer squad?" Deputy Jones asked.

Tessa nodded.

"That doesn't mean he won't start into the next grades," the deputy acknowleged. "Ones above or below. Kind of sounds like he has a gripe, though, with the senior class cheerleaders."

Trace crossed his arms over his chest. "Is there anyone left that you could ask about potential incidents that could have occurred?"

"Between now and tomorrow night," Deputy Jones said, "I'll start running some background checks on some of the guys in your class. Are there any you can think of that we should look at first?"

"Seriously, I must have walked around in a bubble my whole senior year. I thought everyone was happy. And everyone was working toward graduation. We planned a big campout by the bluffs for the night of graduation." Tessa drew in a deep, shaky breath and let it out slowly. "Being teenagers like we were, we knew there would be alcohol. So we collected everybody's keys. Nobody could leave until they'd sobered up in the morning."

Trace nodded. "Smart."

"That's what we thought," Tessa said softly. "We had a bonfire, music and dancing. It was a great party. Alcohol did flow freely. Nobody noticed that Penny was gone. So many of the young couples had gone off into the brush to make out. No one was keeping track."

Irish's lips quirked upward. "Sounds about right."

"We had a lot of pregnancies out of that party. It wasn't until the next afternoon that we heard about Penny. Her parents had alerted the sheriff when she didn't come home that morning."

"Where did they find her?" Irish asked.

"They sent a search party out to the bluff and found her body at the base of a cliff. At first, they assumed she'd wandered off drunk and fallen over the edge." Tessa's voice caught. "Until the autopsy report came in. She had strangulation marks around her neck. We were all shocked. The sheriff's department asked for help from the state crime lab. People came out and questioned every one of the students in the class. No one saw anything. After that night, many of us went on to college. We left Whiskey Gulch for four years. Those who stayed took up a trade, became receptionists in doctor's offices, or married and had children."

"Penny didn't get that opportunity," Irish concluded, his heart hurting for Tessa and the good folks of Whiskey Gulch.

Tessa shook her head.

"Hopefully, doing a background check on the guys in your class, we'll find something. Maybe one of them will have a police record," Deputy Jones said. "Maybe some jail time."

"I know Martha Stevens, Penny's mother. She and my mother were friends," Trace said. "I'll ask Martha if she knew of anything that happened that Penny might have told her. Something that's not already in the police records."

"There's a Josh Kitterman that works at the building supply store. Is he any relation to Kitty Kitterman?" Deputy Jones asked.

Tessa gaze momentarily held the deputy's. "That's her older brother. He joined the military after high school."

"We can stop by the lumber store tomorrow. I need to get supplies to either repair or replace the door to Tessa's bedroom," Irish said.

"I'll spend some time looking through my yearbook, try to remember who might have had a gripe with the cheerleaders," Tessa offered.

"And we'll get everybody in place thirty minutes prior to your meeting with your ex," Trace said. "In the meantime, try to get some rest."

Tessa nodded. "I will. I hope you find something. I feel like I'm living on the edge and that my number will soon be up." She reached up and clasped Irish's hand on her shoulder, then tipped her head toward Trace. "Thank you for loaning Irish to me. I don't know what I would've done without him. I'd probably be dead by now."

"Irish and I served together. He's good at what he

does," Trace said. "I've told him he's to stick with you until this is over."

Tessa laughed without mirth. "I just hope it's not over with my death."

"It won't be," Irish said.

Trace shook hands with Irish. "Stay with her."

Irish smiled. "You don't have to tell me twice."

"We'll leave you guys to your evening," Deputy Jones said. "If you remember anything, don't hesitate to call. I don't care what time of day or night."

"I will," Tessa promised.

Trace and Deputy Jones left. Irish followed them to the door and locked it behind them. He returned to the kitchen where he'd left Tessa seated at the table.

Silent tears slipped from her eyes. "I can't believe I didn't know this. Three women who were my friends in high school, and I didn't know they were dead."

"And now you're the target," Irish said. "I guess you know what that means, don't you?"

"I'm in danger?" Tessa asked. "We already know that."

"It means I'm going to stick to you like a fly on flypaper." His mouth spread wide in a grin.

Her lips twitched. "Sounds uncomfortable, but I'm game."

"I just need to pop these steaks into the oven for a few minutes and chop up a salad. Think you won't starve in the next fifteen minutes?"

"Leave my steak in a little longer. I don't like it to moo."

"One steak well done coming up."

Tessa rose from her chair. "And I can help you cut up the salad."

"You've been on your feet all day. Just sit."

She shook her head and remained standing. "No, I need to move. This is all too much." More tears welled in her eyes and she swiped at them. "I don't know why I keep crying. It doesn't make anything better."

Irish wrapped his arms around her and pulled her against his chest.

"I shouldn't cry," she sobbed.

"Yes, you should," he countered. "They were your friends.

She buried her face against his shirt. "I'm sorry I'm soaking your shirt."

"It's okay. I have another."

For a long moment, they stood together. He stroked her hair and just let her cry. It ripped his heart out to see her so upset. And made him even angrier at the man who'd caused all this. He leaned toward her ex-husband being the one behind the attacks and murders.

The man hadn't been averse to beating his wife. He could harbor enough anger to kill other women. And maybe he hadn't killed his ex-wife because, at the time, they were married. But now that they weren't, he might be targeting her. And since he hadn't been successful so far, setting up a public meeting would draw her out. They'd have to be ready in case he tried to pull a fast one. The more Irish thought about it, the more Irish liked the idea of the metal detector at the door to the diner.

When her tears subsided, he moved her to arm's length and stared down into her red puffy eyes. Even with puffy eyes, she was a beautiful woman. "Come on. Let's get something to eat."

She nodded. "Thank you."

Before he could think better of it, he tipped her chin up and brushed his lips across hers.

Her eyes widened. "Why did you do that?"

"I don't know," Irish said. "It just seemed like the thing to do. And I have been wanting to do it all day."

Her gaze met his. "Would you do it again?" she asked so softly he wasn't sure he'd heard right.

He smiled down at her gently. "Only if you want me to."

Her tongue shot out and swept across her lips.

Irish's pulse quickened. "Do you want me to?"

She gave him a silent nod and lifted up on her toes.

He shook his head. "I shouldn't. You're in a very emotional state. Kissing you would be taking advantage of you. But, hell, I can't resist." He lowered his mouth onto hers and crushed her body against his. At first, his kiss was gentle, but when she opened her mouth to him, he swept in to claim her. For a long time, they remained locked in each other's arms.

When reason returned, Irish lifted his head and drew in a deep breath. "I'm sorry," he said. "I shouldn't have let that happen."

She shook her head. "You didn't let it happen. I asked for it."

"I shouldn't let it happen again," he said.

"Why?" she questioned. "We're both mature adults who can make our own decisions."

"Yeah, but you distract me, woman," he said. "And if I'm distracted, I might miss something. Something that could cost you your life." He set her away from his body and then dropped his hands to his sides. "I have to keep focused."

She smoothed her hands over her T-shirt. "Okay, then. Let's focus on supper."

Irish put the steaks in the oven, and got the lettuce, tomatoes, and other fixings out of the refrigerator. They stood side by side, cutting up vegetables for the salad. All the while he wanted to throw down the knife, take her in his arms and carry her into the bedroom to make passionate love to her. He couldn't keep her safe if he couldn't stay focused. And he couldn't stay focused when he was standing right next to her. Perhaps he should have Trace assign someone else to be her bodyguard.

Tessa tossed the cut tomatoes into the lettuce, glanced up at him and smiled.

In that one look, Irish knew that he was doomed. He couldn't let somebody else take charge of her safety. It was up to him to keep her alive. And he would. Or die trying.

Chapter Nine

Once the steaks were broiled and the potatoes were out of the microwave, Tessa loaded plates with salad, steak, and steaming potatoes, and carried them to the table.

Irish followed her with iced glasses full of tea.

"Doesn't seem right to be eating steaks without candlelight. Hold on." She set her plate down, went back to one of the cabinets, pulled out two candlestick holders and stuck two white tapers in them. She dug in a drawer for a box of matches and handed them over to Irish. "Will you do the honors?"

"It would be my pleasure." He struck a match on the side of the box and lit the two candles. Then he went to the switch on the wall and turned off the lights in the kitchen.

Tessa smiled. "That's better."

"It's almost like a date," Irish commented.

"Except you're my bodyguard, not my date. But it is nice to have some ambience." Tessa handed him a steak knife.

"Yeah, and if it were a date," Irish said, "I would

have sprung for the filet mignon instead of the top sirloin."

Tessa puffed out her chest. "Actually, you're in luck here because I prefer the top sirloin to the filet. They're not quite as thick and I can get it cooked all the way through."

Irish grinned. "I'd call that lucky."

"If this were a real date, where would you take me?" Tessa asked.

"Actually, I kind of like it right here. But since it's your place and I'm living in the bunkhouse, I would probably take you to a nice little restaurant with cozy atmosphere. Some place we can be alone but not alone. Not some place that's loud with a lot of music. I like music, but I like more to get to know the woman I take out on a date. And you can't do that when you have to talk over music. I'm not saying that after dinner I wouldn't take her dancing. I've been known to have a mean two-step on the dance floor."

"I take it you mean that you would be going to a dance hall," Tessa said.

"I can dance to rock or pop music," Irish said. "But I prefer country-western because I get to hold the woman in my arms."

A shiver of awareness caught Tessa off guard. She knew what it was like to have Irish's arms around her when she was scared. But dancing? Dancing could be a prelude to something more. Heat coiled at her core.

"Did your ex ever take you dancing?"

She gave a crooked smile. "Only to the prom. And only because he was going to be crowned the home-

Treat Yourself with 2 Free Books!

Suspense

Suspenseful Romance

GET UP TO 4 FREE BOOKS & 2 FREE GIFTS WORTH OVER $20

See Inside For Details

Claim Them While You Can

Get ready to relax and indulge with your **FREE BOOKS** and more!

Claim up to FOUR NEW BOOKS & TWO MYSTERY GIFTS – absolutely FREE!

Dear Reader,

We both know life can be difficult at times. That's why it's important to treat yourself so you can relax and recharge once in a while.

And I'd like to help you do this by sending you this amazing offer of up to FOUR brand new full length FREE BOOKS that WE pay for.

This is everything I have ready to send to you right now:

Try **Harlequin® Romantic Suspense** books featuring heart-racing page-turners with unexpected plot twists and irresistible chemistry that will keep you guessing to the very end.

Try **Harlequin Intrigue® Larger-Print** books featuring action-packed stories that will keep you on the edge of your seat. Solve the crime and deliver justice at all costs.
Or **TRY BOTH!**

All we ask in return is that you answer 4 simple questions on the attached Treat Yourself survey. You'll get **Two Free Books** and **Two Mystery Gifts** from each series you try, *altogether worth over $20*! Who could pass up a deal like that?

Sincerely,

Pam Powers

Harlequin Reader Service

Treat Yourself to Free Books and Free Gifts.

Answer 4 fun questions and get rewarded.

We love to connect with our readers!
Please tell us a little about you...

	YES	NO
1. I LOVE reading a good book.	◯	◯
2. I indulge and "treat" myself often.	◯	◯
3. I love getting FREE things.	◯	◯
4. Reading is one of my favorite activities.	◯	◯

TREAT YOURSELF • Pick your 2 Free Books...

Yes! Please send me my Free Books from each series I select and Free Mystery Gifts. I understand that I am under no obligation to buy anything, as explained on the back of this card.

Which do you prefer?

❑ **Harlequin® Romantic Suspense** 240/340 HDL GRCZ
❑ **Harlequin Intrigue® Larger-Print** 199/399 HDL GRCZ
❑ **Try Both** 240/340 & 199/399 HDL GRDD

FIRST NAME	LAST NAME

ADDRESS

APT.#	CITY

STATE/PROV.	ZIP/POSTAL CODE

EMAIL ❑ Please check this box if you would like to receive newsletters and promotional emails from Harlequin Enterprises ULC and its affiliates. You can unsubscribe anytime.

HI/HRS-520-TY22

coming king. We danced one dance and that was it. It was the obligatory royal dance."

"And let me guess," Irish said. "You love to dance, don't you?"

She nodded. "As a cheerleader we choreographed tumbling and dance routines, but that's dancing by yourself or with the team. It's not as intimate."

Irish nodded. "That's what I'm talking about. A date should be intimate. What did you do on your dates with Randy?" He held up his hands. "You don't have to answer that. That's too personal and none of my business."

"It's okay." Tessa laughed. "Seems like we were always out with groups—other members of the football team...cheerleaders. Randy liked an audience. Granted, as a cheerleader, so did I. But after high school, I learned that relationships were more important than audiences. I had to work hard to make the grades I needed to get into nursing school. My study group became my family. My friends were very important to me. They helped me get through it. I wasn't a cheerleader in college. I didn't stand in front of everybody. I didn't have an audience."

"You said Randy went to different colleges," Irish said.

"He did. On a football scholarship. He was right back into the same situation he'd had in high school. He had an audience and he played for it. Up until his junior year when he injured his rotator cuff and he couldn't throw the football anymore."

Irish shook his head. "That had to set him back."

"His folks hired a tutor to get him through the rest of his studies to graduate with a business degree. They had friends in San Antonio who hired him as a manager. After he lost his position on the football team—"

"He lost his audience," Irish finished.

Tessa nodded. "I think he came back to Whiskey Gulch to marry me in some misguided attempt to reclaim some of his past fame."

"Or he knew you were a good catch."

"I'd concentrated on making good grades. While going to college, I didn't have time for relationships. When I came back to Whiskey Gulch, it just seemed like the thing to do, to marry my high school sweetheart. I'd accomplished my educational goals. It was time to start my life goals of having a family and raising children. I thought Randy had the same goals. I didn't realize it was important to actually talk through life goals with your potential spouse before you marry."

"What were his goals?" Irish asked.

Tessa snorted. "Well, it sure wasn't having children. To him, life was always a competition. In football, it was a competition to be the best. In track, it was competition to be the best. In the business that he was hired into, he strove to be the best. He learned to play golf so that he could play with the bigwigs. He moved up the corporate ladder pretty quickly."

"In the meantime, what did you do?" Irish asked.

"I went to work in a clinic so that I could be home in the evening to make dinner for him or to go out as his pretty little wife—his arm-candy—to all the functions where the executive officers would notice him. Once again, he liked being the center of attention.

"And he was good at it, until his immediate boss realized that he was jockeying for his position. He had him transferred to a dark corner of the building, calling it a growth experience that he needed in order to move up the ladder. Every time he tried to get the attention of his boss's superior, his boss found a way to get in between them and stop him. Randy came home angrier and angrier, and he took it out on me."

"He became violent," Irish said.

"It started by him criticizing everything I did from what I cooked for dinner to what I wore. He didn't like how I fixed my hair or my makeup. He blamed me for the demotion saying that it reflected poorly on him because I didn't go to as many of the functions as I should have. I hadn't supported him in his profession. Never mind that I had a job of my own where I was on my feet most of the day and was tired when I got home. The man really should have been a lawyer. He was good at making me believe the garbage he fed me. It was all my fault. I believed it. I thought it was my fault that he didn't want to have children. I wasn't pretty enough. I wasn't good in bed."

"How do you figure?" Irish said.

She laughed. "He told me I was an ice queen. I would go to sleep before he even got to the bed. I wasn't passionate enough."

"Couldn't he see that you were exhausted?" Irish asked.

Tessa stared down at her untouched food. "I was exhausted, and I thought it was my fault that I was exhausted. I went to the doctor I worked for and asked him to run a CBC panel to see if I had low iron, or low something, that was causing me to always be so tired. All of that came back normal. I was healthy. He suggested I go see a marriage counselor.

"When I brought that up with Randy, he blew his top. That's when he hit me the first time. He said he didn't need a counselor. If anybody needed it, it was me. I was the one who was at fault. Again, I believed him. I believed all of his brainwashing. I deserved to be hit."

Irish shook his head. "No woman deserves to be hit."

She smiled. "I know that now. I should have seen the signs. Randy's boss was determined to get rid of him. When it finally happened, and they eliminated his position, Randy was so angry. He came home, picked a fight with me over the dinner I'd made, drank too much bourbon and then used me as a punching bag. He left me unconscious on the kitchen floor." Tessa glanced up.

Irish's face was as hard as a rock. His jaw was so tight, it twitched.

"I'm not telling you all this so you'll feel sorry for me. I want you to understand why I don't want to see him. I also want you to understand why I don't want you to do anything violent against him, even though he might deserve it."

Irish's fists clenched so tightly, the knuckles turned white.

Her eyes narrowed. "Promise me."

That twitch in his jaw kept jerking. He didn't say anything for a few moments. Then he let out a breath. "Okay, I promise. But I won't let him hurt you."

"Thank you. I learned something else from Randy. That violence for the sake of violence is never the answer. It's taken these past six months and lots of therapy sessions to come to the conclusion that I was not the one at fault. And it's taken me that long not to flinch when a man touches me."

Irish's eyes widened. "I've touched you."

She smiled. "Yes, you have. And I didn't flinch."

"Geez, Tessa. If I ever do anything that makes you cringe or feel uncomfortable, tell me. I'll stop doing it immediately, and I won't blame you. What you went through, what you're going through, is a form of PTSD. It is not unlike what some soldiers who've been captured and tortured by the enemy have gone through. It can take years before the nightmares fade."

Tessa nodded. "That's what my therapist told me." She lifted her fork and cut into her steak. "But enough about me. What about you? What was it like in the war?" She popped the bite of steak into her mouth.

"That's a pretty broad question," he said, and stared across the table at her.

"If you could sum it up in one word, what would that one word be?" She gave him a crooked smile. "My therapist used that one on me."

He continued chewing and swallowed before he answered. "Intense."

Tessa looked back down at her plate, shook her head and laughed. "While my ex was stressing over a management position, you and your teammates were more worried about living through the night. That's real stress. But, really, what was it like? Being a part of Delta Force?"

As his gaze held hers across the table in the candlelight, he spoke one word, "Family."

Tessa's hand curled around her napkin.

"Those men, my team, were my brothers," Irish said. "I would have done anything for them."

"But you left Delta Force?" Tessa challenged.

He nodded. "I did. And not a day goes by that I don't second-guess myself. Should I have stayed? If I had stayed, would it have made a difference between life and death for someone? Does my team feel abandoned? Could I have saved more lives out in the field?"

He stared at the flame burning on the end of the candle. "I'm sitting here in the candlelight with a beautiful woman, while my team could be out in some hellhole, fighting against an enemy they may or may not be able to see. All because I wanted a chance to start the rest of my life. I didn't want to wait until I retired. Hell, I might be too old," he laughed. "I almost waited too long."

Tessa frowned. "What do you mean?"

"A week before I was supposed to deploy back to the States to process out, we had to go on a mission. We make jokes about short-timers, but it's true. More often than not, when a soldier or a unit has to perform a mission close to the date they're supposed to ship home, you're almost guaranteed that something bad will happen."

Tessa's frown deepened. "And did it?"

Irish nodded. "I was injured and almost didn't make it out. If it hadn't been for my teammates, I wouldn't have. They didn't give up on me. And to top it off, when we got back to our base, there was an MP waiting for us. He was there to deliver news to Trace Travis that his father had been murdered."

"I heard about that. What an awful tragedy. Mr. Travis was a good man." Tessa's gaze dropped to her hand. "And the rest of your team?"

"They survived the mission. And they've gone on without the two of us. To them, it's just another day in the life of a Delta Force soldier. Two fresh, green, Delta Force soldiers would join the team and take our place."

Tessa covered his hand with hers. "You may feel like you're letting them down by not being with them, but you're needed here. I need you. If you hadn't had my back, I would be dead now."

He turned his hand over and gripped hers. "Whatever happens tomorrow night, I'll be there. I won't let anyone hurt you."

"I believe that. And not because you're saying

it." Tessa squeezed his hand. "Randy said a lot of things he didn't mean. And I believed his words. But I learned that actions speak a lot louder than words, and your actions have been honorable. And, by the way, this steak is delicious. We should finish before it gets cold."

His lips twisted. "You're right. We should eat."

Tessa ate a few more bites of her baked potato, her salad, and her steak before she gave up and set her fork beside her plate.

"Not tender enough for you?" Irish asked.

She shook her head. "I'm exhausted."

"Then I'll take care of the dishes, you go on to bed."

She yawned, covering her mouth with her hand. "I'm going to take you up on that. A man who will do the dishes is priceless. You sure know how to sweep a girl off her feet on a first date."

"You should see me on a second date. I might even scrub the bathrooms. I'm quite good at cleaning latrines. The army taught me that particular skill."

"Thank you for sharing your experience with me," Tessa said. "It puts my life in perspective."

He stood, held out his hand, and waited for her to place hers in his. "I'm so sorry for what you went through."

She stepped closer. "I know."

He cupped her cheek and brushed his thumb across her lips. "I can't imagine anyone wanting to hit this beautiful face."

"And I can't imagine the horrors you must have

faced in battle." Tessa raised her free hand to cover his on her face. And she turned to press a kiss to his palm.

Irish tensed. "Your lips were meant for kissing."

She smiled shyly. "I'd be amenable to that idea."

He shook his head. "I can't."

Tessa frowned. "Can't?"

"If I were to kiss you, I'd lose all focus," he said. "I need to retain my focus, or I might miss something that could mean the difference between life and death."

For a long moment, Tessa stared up at Irish's face, wanting so much more but not willing to push him into something he might not want as badly.

"Okay, then." She stepped back until his hand dropped to his side, turned, and hobbled out of the room. Her cheeks burned. She felt foolish for throwing herself at the man. If he'd really wanted to kiss her, he would have. Now she'd have to be content to go to bed and dream about a kiss that she'd never have.

IRISH'S GAZE FOLLOWED Tessa until she disappeared down the hallway. It had taken every ounce of determination not to kiss her, when every fiber of his being wanted to. The woman needed a protector. Not a man taking advantage of her distress. She'd been physically and emotionally abused by her ex. She didn't need a man confusing her while she was still working through her issues.

He went to work on cleaning the dishes and putting food away. When he was done, he stepped outside the house and stared up at the stars.

This was the perfect night to take a woman out on a date. A clear, Texas night with an infinite amount of stars. And the ones he would stare at the most would be the ones reflected in her eyes.

Maybe after this was over, after her attacker was caught, he might ask Tessa out on a real date. He'd take it slowly, make sure she was comfortable and that she knew without a doubt that he would never hurt her like her ex-husband had. Until then, he'd be strictly hands-off. He made a pass around the house, checking that everything was secure on the outside, even testing the back door to make sure that it was locked before he came back through the main entrance.

He paused in front of her bedroom door.

"Tessa?" When she didn't answer, he pushed the door open. A light burned on her nightstand and she lay against the sheets, her cheek resting in the palm of her hand. Her eyes were closed and she was breathing deeply. She was asleep.

Irish returned to the living room, sat on the couch and then stretched out, laying his head on the pillow. He hadn't felt too exhausted, but as soon as he closed his eyes, he was out.

He wasn't sure how long he slept, but a soft sound woke him in the middle of the night. It sounded suspiciously like someone sobbing. And then it stopped. He lay there for a moment, waiting for it to start again so that he could figure out where it was coming from.

A moment later Tessa appeared in her doorway, carrying her pillow and a blanket.

"Are you okay?" he asked.

She shook her head.

He patted the couch beside him. "Come here."

She limped across the living room and sat on the edge of the cushion.

"Bad dream?"

Again, she nodded. "I was back in the willow trees. Instead of a man attacking me, the willow branches wrapped around me." She shivered. "They pulled me in, suffocating me."

"Sounds creepy," Irish said. He turned on his side and scooted as far back as he could against the couch cushions. "You're welcome to join me." He lifted his head while she positioned her pillow next to his and then they both laid down. Her back to him. Her hand resting beneath her cheek.

"I'm not asking you to kiss me," she said. "But would you put your arm around me? I feel safer when you do."

He draped his arm across her middle and pulled her close. With her nestled against him, sleep was the furthest thing from his mind. He fought to control his body's natural reaction to hers pressed to his. It took a great amount of effort, but somehow he managed.

"Irish?" Tessa asked.

"Mmm," he responded.

"Have you ever been in love?"

He chuckled. Her question was unexpected and he wasn't sure how to answer. "I thought I was once."

"What was she like?" Tessa asked.

"She had curly red hair and green eyes."

"Oh," Tessa said. "Are you partial to red hair and green eyes?"

"I was back then."

"What happened?"

He laughed again. "When I tried to kiss her, she slapped my face and told me boys were weird. I got sent home from school that day. And I never tried to kiss a girl on the playground again."

"How old were you?" Tessa giggled.

He laughed. "I was in first grade. I swear that incident scarred me for life."

"Surely not." She turned to look over her shoulder. "You can't tell me you've been celibate all of this time."

"No, I can't tell you that." He swept her hair back from her temple. "I've dated other women. And I've kissed a few. But I've never been in love. I was afraid to let myself get that attached while I was with Delta Force."

"Afraid?" she whispered. "I can't imagine you being afraid of anything."

"I've had a few close calls where I've been afraid," he said. "I'm only human."

"In battle or in relationships?"

"Both."

Tessa laid her arm over his around her middle.

"Now that you're not in Delta Force, do you think you'll let yourself fall in love?"

Not only did he think he would, he k*new* he would. He wanted to start the rest of his life. He wanted a family. He wanted children. He wanted a wife to come home to.

"Eventually," he said.

"Irish…" Tessa started.

"Go to sleep Tessa."

"Sorry," Tessa said, "sometimes I talk too much."

By morning, he would be exhausted. But for now, he reveled in the opportunity to hold her. To smell the fragrance of her hair. To feel the softness of her body against his. In the morning, he'd put some distance between them again.

Chapter Ten

Tessa slept better than she'd slept since she'd left San Antonio. She awoke to a warm arm around her mid-section and lay for a moment, basking in a feeling of well-being. And something more. She'd asked Irish if he'd ever been in love, mostly because she had wondered what it felt like. She'd thought herself in love with Randy, but what she'd had with Randy had been high school infatuation that lasted into college, only because she hadn't had time to pursue another relationship. Yes, she felt warm and safe with Irish. And yes, she wanted to kiss him. Heck, she wanted more than just to kiss him.

An electric current rippled throughout her body.

Was it just physical attraction, or was it love? Could someone fall in love in just a couple of days? She'd heard of love at first sight, but she'd never been convinced that it really existed.

She wasn't sure what she was feeling for Irish. But it felt good. She lay for a few minutes longer as the sun peeked its way through the blinds in the front window. Irish had said he'd wanted to keep his distance so that he could retain his focus. Was it more than that? Was he not as attracted to her as she was to him? He'd said that he'd wanted to kiss her. A strong virile man like Irish would follow his instincts, wouldn't he?

Tessa sighed. All she knew was she couldn't keep throwing herself at him. She needed to give him the space he desired. And she wasn't doing that by lying next to him on the couch.

Moving slowly, she slipped out from beneath his arm and rolled quietly off the couch onto her hands and knees. She turned to note that Irish's eyes were still closed and his chest was moving in slow, steady breaths. Afraid she'd wake him, she crawled away from the couch before she stood and hurried to her bedroom, closing the door softly behind her. Tessa dressed quickly in jeans and a soft white T-shirt. Then she entered the bathroom, brushed her teeth, combed her hair straight and pulled it into a loose ponytail at the back of her neck. She applied a little blush to her pale cheeks, and some mascara to her eyelashes, and just a touch of rose-colored lipstick to her lips. Satisfied that she didn't look pale and pasty, she applied a fresh Band-Aid to her heel, and slipped on a pair of socks and shoes. When she was finished, she eased open her bedroom door and looked out at an empty couch.

So much for not waking him. The scent of coffee drifted to her and she followed it to its source.

Irish stood in the kitchen barefoot, his T-shirt untucked, and a five-o'clock shadow on his chin. Tessa took a moment to appreciate the view. The man had no clue how attractive he was. He made her heart flutter every time she saw him.

He turned and smiled when he saw her. "Do you want your eggs scrambled or fried this time?"

"Why don't you let me cook?" she said.

"Tired of my cooking already?" he asked.

"Far from it," she said. "But I like to pull my weight. I think we have enough ingredients to make omelets. How would you like that?" she asked.

"Sounds good. I can chop, while you man the skillet."

She smiled. "Deal."

Once again, they worked side by side, preparing a meal together. To Tessa, it felt as natural as breathing. They seemed to anticipate each other's needs, moving in unison to make two golden, fluffy omelets full of tasty vegetables.

While Tessa scooped the omelets out of the frying pan onto the plates, Irish filled glasses with orange juice and set them on the table, along with forks and knives. Tessa carried their plates to the table and set them across the table from each other.

When she started to take her seat, Irish held her chair for her, something Randy never did, unless others were watching.

"I could get used to having you around," she said. "It's a lot more fun to cook when you have help."

"I like to cook," Irish said. "It beats the heck out of chow hall food."

"I can only imagine," Tessa said.

They ate their breakfast talking about football teams and the livestock out at the Whiskey Gulch Ranch. Irish made her laugh when he discussed the different personalities of the horses in the barn and pastures. He made each one sound human, like friends. Some were gentle and others were full of sass. And he smiled a lot when he talked about them.

"You really like working with the livestock out at the ranch, don't you?" Tessa asked.

He nodded. "I'm living the dream. I promised myself when I left active duty that I'd go to work with animals for a while before I pursued my other dream of home and family."

"Sounds like you landed in the right spot then," Tessa said.

"I don't think it would have happened if Trace's father hadn't been murdered. When I knew Trace on active duty, he talked about staying the full twenty or more. He never mentioned home. He didn't talk about his family, except for maybe his mother. From what he's said, there were bad feelings between him and his father. I think he regrets that he didn't have a chance to clear those feelings before his father was murdered."

"That is too bad," Tessa said. "I remember Mr. Travis did a lot for the community. He was well respected by so many."

"Trace had the option of going back on active duty, but he chose to stay and run the ranch. I wouldn't be here now if he hadn't made that decision to remain in Whiskey Gulch and set up his security business. He knew how hard it was for folks coming off active duty. After living in a war zone, the transition can be pretty rough. He wanted to give people separating from the military a purpose, utilizing some of the skills they had learned while in the military."

"It's a good thing that he came back to stay," Tessa said.

"He's giving his brothers-in-arms a place to work, helping people like me. And he's carrying on his father's legacy in his own way. Trace Travis is a good man, and his security business concept is admirable. Now, if we could just surface some clues, figure out who's after you and neutralize him, we can prove out the business concept."

Tessa's eyes narrowed. "Speaking of clues, I think I have an old yearbook. Let me get it out."

Irish nodded toward her plate. "Finish your omelet first, while it's hot. You need food to fuel your body. We don't know what we might face today."

She quickly cleaned her plate and carried it to the sink. Then she left Irish in the kitchen to go into the hallway where a bookshelf held old photo albums and yearbooks.

Tessa returned to the kitchen with a yearbook. She opened the book to the seniors and ran her fingers across the photographs. She pointed to a picture of a smiling brunette. "That's Penny." She turned the page and pointed to Kitty Kitterman. Turning the page once more, she pointed to an image of a pretty girl with blond hair. "And this is Bethany York."

Irish turned the pages back to the first one. "And there you are. You haven't changed much since high school."

"I have a few more crow's feet, and I've lost some of the muscle mass I acquired with all the gymnastics we did."

"But you still look the same," Irish said. "Your hair's a little shorter. That's really the only difference."

One by one, Tessa pointed out each of the guys in her senior class. Her finger paused on Randy. "He was the most handsome boy in the senior class," she muttered. "Not that looks mean anything, it's what's inside that counts." She laughed. "I learned that about Randy as well as myself."

"I understand about Randy, but what do you mean that you learned that about yourself?"

"I relied on my looks in high school." She glanced up with a twisted smile. "My looks didn't save me from the beatings in my marriage. I had to find the strength from within to leave him."

ANGER BURNED IN Irish's gut. If he didn't control it, he might break his promise to Tessa—not to hurt Randy that night when he saw him. He pulled himself back to the task of looking through her yearbook.

"You say Randy was a football player," Irish said. She nodded. "The quarterback."

"And the guy that attacked you—" Irish frowned "—was bigger than Randy?"

"I could swear he was bigger than Randy," she

said. "Even after college and losing his football scholarship, Randy liked to stay in shape. He had no tolerance for people who let themselves go."

Irish shook his head. "Is that why you jog? Did he badger you into working out so you wouldn't get fat?"

"Partly," she admitted. "But mostly because, when I'm jogging, I'm staying active. I don't have time to dwell on the failures in my life. And it generates endorphins and helps to cheer me when I'm down."

"Exercise has that added bonus." He glanced at the yearbook. "Which of the guys in your class were big guys?"

Tessa moved through the senior class pictures alphabetically. "Mike Bradley was one of the tallest guys on the team. He was on the offensive line. At six-four, he weighed over two hundred pounds, and he was hard to get around. He protected the quarterback."

Irish grimaced. "Is he still in Whiskey Gulch?"

Tessa smiled. "He is. He became the coach at the middle school. And he teaches history. He married while he was in college. His wife teaches at the elementary school. They have two small children."

A wife and kids didn't mean he wasn't capable of hurting someone else. "Did he ever have anger issues?"

Again, Tessa smiled. "Mike is a big teddy bear of a guy and one of the nicest human beings you'll ever meet."

Unconvinced, Irish shook his head. "You never

know. Sometimes those nice guys are hiding things, even from their families."

"Not Mike, he was always an open book. And would do anything for anybody. He and his wife make the cutest couple. He's so big. She's so small. And they look genuinely happy. Mike isn't our guy." Tessa moved her finger to the next guy. "This is Connor Daniels. He was a football player as well. Not nearly as tall as Mike Bradley, though. He, too, was on the offensive line, and sometimes he played the position of running back. He was fast, on the field and with the girls."

"Still in town?" Irish asked.

Tessa nodded. "And he seems to have straightened out a lot. He trained to become a firefighter, and now he works for the town of Whiskey Gulch as one of the few full-time firefighters. One of the ladies I work with at the hospital, Allison, is dating a firefighter who works with Connor. He only has good things to say about him. I think he's dating Sadie Green, who works as a waitress at the truck stop along the interstate."

"It might be worth our time to talk to his girlfriend. She might feel differently than his coworker."

"Maybe."

"How do you know so much about all these people if you've been away for a while?" Irish asked.

With a slight grin, Tessa shrugged. "Hospital gossip and it's a small town." She moved on to the next guy. "That's Nathan Harris, also a football player. A linebacker. He worked on defensive line."

Irish studied the man in the picture. Harris had a

big face, brown hair, brown eyes, heavy eyebrows and a square jaw. "How tall was he?" Irish asked.

"Over six feet, and he was big-boned. And surprisingly fast for as big as he was. He made amazing tackles in some of our games."

"Does he still live in Whiskey Gulch?" Irish asked.

"I'm not sure about him, but his mother still lives here. I think he's a truck driver. He's got to be on the road more often than not."

"What was he like in high school?"

Tessa shrugged. "I don't remember much about him. Seems like he was there, on the fringe of the popular group, and kind of quiet. I don't remember him saying much." She slid her finger to the right, landing on a teen with dirty-blond hair and gray eyes. "That's Eddy Knowlton. About the same height as Nathan. He got hit hard in the last football game of the season. He had a concussion and I think it scrambled his brain a little bit. He's never been quite the same."

"Where is he now?" Irish asked.

"He works as a janitor at the hospital where I work."

Irish didn't like the sound of that. If he was the one behind the attacks, he had easy access to Tessa at work. "Do you think he's capable of attacking a woman?"

"I don't know," Tessa said. "Every time I see him in the hallway he's moving slowly, pushing a mop or a broom. He always keeps his head down and never smiles. I feel bad for him. He had so much going for him until that injury."

Irish knew head injuries did funny things to some people. He'd seen it in soldiers with Traumatic Brain Injuries. "Was he at the party the night of graduation?"

Tessa nodded. "Yeah, everybody was." Tessa turned the page and pointed to another male. "That's Wayne Payton. Talk about a guy that had anger issues." The young man had black hair, brown eyes, and appeared heavyset. "He was another offensive lineman, who occasionally played dirty and hurt the members of other teams. He's still in town, but he's working as a cable guy. He runs internet and TV lines around here."

"Which means he has access to people's houses."

Tessa nodded. "Yeah, but only when they let him in. He doesn't have keys to people's houses."

"Is he married?"

She shook her head. "No. He was married to Marcie Williamson, but that didn't last. They married right after she graduated high school. She divorced him within a year. She supports herself on the tips she makes as a waitress at the diner. She and Penny were good friends, and Penny's murder almost did her in."

"We should talk to her," Irish said.

"I know the police questioned her at length after Penny's death. They spoke to a lot of us that were at the party. Marcie was a year younger than us, also on the cheer squad, but a junior. She came to the party the night of the graduation with Wayne. I guess she got pretty drunk, because she doesn't remember when Penny wandered off or went missing. I never got the whole story from her."

Tessa's finger moved to the next image of a guy with light brown hair and brown eyes. "That's Hayden Severs. He was our receiver and our best running back. The guy was not that big, but he could run fast. And if Randy got the ball anywhere close to them, you could be guaranteed that Hayden would catch it."

"How tall was he?"

"Mmm, probably about five-ten. He was lean then and still is. He works for an autobody shop in town. And drives a tow truck."

"What about this guy?" Irish pointed to a young man with glasses.

Tessa smiled. "That's Wally, or Richard Wallace. He was the class geek. He ran the computer lab." She frowned. "He had the biggest crush on Penny. I remember the sheriff grilled him with questions. But he had a rock-solid alibi. He was not at the party that night. He was celebrating graduation with some of his geek friends, playing that retro game—Dungeons and Dragons—at the local church. There were at least three witnesses who attested to the fact that they played through the night."

"Who else in your class, or maybe a lower class, was big enough to be the man who attacked you?"

Tessa pointed to a few pictures of some of the guys in the junior class. After a while, she looked up. "I don't know what to tell you. It's been years since I've seen some of these people. Some of them I see every day. None of the men I know stand out as potential attackers. I tend to see the good in most people. But then, I thought Randy was a nice guy... until I married him. You see why I don't trust my own judgement?"

Irish smiled at her. "It's not a bad thing to see the good in most people."

"No, it's not." Tessa sighed. "But it leaves me open to be taken advantage of."

"Yes, it does." He glanced at the clock on the wall. "Let's go to the lumber store and see if we can find Josh Kitterman and ask him about his sister."

She thumbed through a few pages. "Let's do it. All these months I've been living in Whiskey Gulch, I've seen Josh maybe three or four times. I haven't really stopped to talk to him. I didn't realize his sister had been murdered. I thought she was happily living somewhere else. Happily married, unlike me. I feel bad that I haven't said anything to him. I've been wallowing in my own misery of a failed marriage when others have had it worse."

"Yours wasn't a case of a failed marriage," Irish said. "It was a case of a successful escape."

She gave him a crooked grin. "When you put it that way, you're right. Let's go see Josh." She closed the yearbook and stood.

"How's that foot?" Irish asked.

"It only hurts a little bit," she admitted. "I'm able

to get around a lot better. Thanks to a certain Delta Force guy who's good at treating wounds."

"Glad I could be of assistance," he said with a bow. "It just puts me one step closer to achieving my status of knight in shining armor. I hope soon I'll be qualified to rescue damsels in distress."

She laughed. "You're already there. This damsel is quite satisfied with your work."

He held out his hand and she placed hers in his. Together, they walked to the front door. Tessa grabbed her purse on the way through the living room. Irish took the keys from her and locked the cottage.

Chapter Eleven

Irish insisted on taking his truck, reasoning that it was bigger, and if there was somebody that wanted to ram into them, it would hold up better than her SUV. The drive to the hardware store took less than five minutes. Irish could appreciate the benefits of living in a small town. It didn't take long to get where he needed go.

Irish pulled into the parking lot, shifted into Park, and climbed down, hurrying around the front of the vehicle to open the door for Tessa. He helped her down from the truck. She took his hand as they walked into the store. It was the first time that she'd reached for him. It made him feel strangely warm and content.

Once inside, Tessa leaned toward Irish. "That's Josh, behind the counter."

Three people stood in line, waiting their turn to check out in front of the man she'd indicated was Josh.

Irish tipped his head toward the rows of hardware and paint supplies. "While we wait for the line to clear, let's get something to repair that hole in the door. Unless you'd rather replace it?"

She shook her head. "I still owe you for the back door. If we can repair the bedroom door, I'm fine with that."

"Should be able to with a little putty and paint. And I found the hole where the bullet actually hit the wall and embedded in it. We could use a little toothpaste or plaster to fill that hole and then just a little touchup paint should cover it completely."

They were standing in the aisle with the wood putty when Tessa whispered, "That's Wayne Payton."

"The cable guy?" Irish studied the guy. He was big, maybe a couple inches taller than Irish himself. And heavyset. "He was the one who dated Marcie, Penny's friend, who was a cheerleader in the class below yours?"

Tessa smiled. "That's the one. He was at the party with Marcie the night Penny died."

"Did he have an alibi?"

"Marcie." Tessa glanced up at Irish. "Should we go question him?"

"Why not? We're here."

What were the chances he'd up and confess to three murders and some attacks on Tessa? Irish thought. He could tell a lot from a person's expression. Maybe the man wouldn't confess in words, but his face might show some of his guilt if he was, indeed, the culprit.

Tessa squared her shoulders and walked with Irish

toward Marcie's ex. "Hey, Wayne," Tessa said. "It's been a long time."

The man's eyes narrowed as he stared at her. "I heard you were back in town." He dipped his head at Irish. "This your new boyfriend, since you dumped Randy?"

Tessa's brow twisted. "Is that what he told you?"

Wayne shrugged. "Not actually. Randy said that he dumped you."

Tessa's lips turned up in the corners. "Sounds like Randy," she muttered beneath her breath.

"I figured it was probably you dumping him," Wayne said. "That's what women seem to do. Marriage vows don't mean squat nowadays."

"I lived up to my side of the union," Tessa said, "until he stopped living up to his. That part about *cherish*? Randy had no clue. And he was well on his way to fulfilling the *'til death do us part*, with me being the one to die."

"That's not what he said. He said you were cheating on him." His gaze shifted to Irish.

"Believe what you want," Tessa said, a hand on Irish's arm to keep him from stepping toward Wayne. His fist clenched. "I heard you and Marcie split up," Tessa said, deflecting Wayne's attack on hers and Randy's marriage.

Wayne snarled.

"Were you of the same line of thought that Randy was?" she asked. "That a wife should be beaten regularly to keep her in line?"

Wayne squared his broad shoulders. "I never laid

a hand on Marcie. She was the one who asked for the divorce. She never got over her best friend's death. After Penny was murdered, she was never the same. I married her anyway, hoping that we could make a life together. She felt guilty that Penny died that night, and she blamed me."

Tessa stiffened beside Irish. "Did you kill Penny?"

"No," Wayne said. "But you would have thought I did. I insisted that Marcie and I make out during the party. And because of that, she left Penny alone. If Marcie and I had not been making out, Penny wouldn't be dead. Therefore, I'm at fault. I might as well have killed Penny, based on the way Marcie was thinking."

"But she married you," Tessa said.

"Yeah. I thought that it would work out. That she'd eventually get over it, and that the wedding would take her mind off Penny's death. And it did for a while. For that whole year that she was a senior, while I was waiting for her to graduate, she stayed busy planning our wedding." Wayne shoved a hand through his hair. "But after we married and settled into our own home, she had too much time on her hands to think about Penny. Our marriage fell apart. I even offered to go see a marriage counselor with her. She refused. Eventually, she filed for divorce."

His shoulders slumped. "The sad thing is, I still love her. I had every intention of living the rest of my life with her. Growing old, having grandchildren, the whole works. All that ended when Penny was murdered." He inhaled a deep breath and let it out. "Look, I don't know what happened between you and Randy, but I know he could be a real jerk when he wanted to be. And you were never anything but nice to me. I'm sorry about what I said. I'm sure you had good reasons for your divorce." He glanced at the watch on his wrist. "I've said enough. Now, I have to go. I'm supposed to be at work." Wayne walked away. He set the items he had in his hands on a shelf and left the store, his shoulders still slumped.

"Do you believe what he said?" Irish asked.

Tessa nodded. "I do. He appears to really regret having lost Marcie. And Marcie vouched for him that night. It wouldn't hurt to talk to Marcie again," Tessa said. "We could stop by the diner at lunch and see if she's working."

"Sounds like a plan." Irish glanced at the counter. Josh was still busy with two other customers.

Tessa touched his arm. "Hey, there's Nathan Harris."

Irish chuckled. "Is that all we have to do is come to the hardware store to run into every male classmate? Is it the social Mecca of Whiskey Gulch?"

"Apparently." Tessa chewed on her bottom lip. "I have no idea how to approach Nathan. He was never easy to talk to and I have nothing in common with him."

"Let me handle it," Irish said.

He approached Nathan. "Excuse me. You from around here?"

Nathan frowned. "Yeah."

Irish smiled. "I don't suppose you know someone who can do some minor repairs around a house, do you?"

Nathan turned to fully face Irish. "Maybe." He looked past Irish to where Tessa stood and nodded. "Tessa."

"Nathan." Tessa gave him a tight smile. "I didn't know you still lived here."

"Never moved," he said. "Once Dad passed, I stayed around the house to help Mom out."

Tessa nodded. "I bet she's glad to have you around."

He nodded. "I don't hear any complaints. What about you? How long have you been back? Haven't seen you around much."

Tessa lifted a shoulder and let it fall. "Other than jogging, going to the grocery store and work, I pretty much stay close to my home."

Nathan lifted his chin. "Mom told me she heard through the grapevine that you ran into some trouble."

Tessa nodded. "Yes, I did."

"Someone attacked you out by the river?" Nathan shook his head. "Sorry to hear that," he said. "I just got back in town late last night."

"Have you been traveling?" Tessa asked.

He shook his head. "I drive a truck. That's probably why you haven't seen me around much. I'm usually on the road."

"How's that working out for you?" Tessa asked.

Nathan shrugged. "It pays the bills, keeps me

busy, and I come back often enough to help out Mom."

"Do you miss our high school days and playing football?" Tessa asked.

Nathan shook his head. "Not really. Football's a tough sport. It's hard on the body. And I don't miss all the drama of high school."

"Any drama in particular?" Tessa asked.

He shook his head. "Just all of it. I was never so glad to put a place behind me."

"You ever marry?" Tessa asked.

He shook his head. "Most women want a man who's home every night. I can't guarantee that in my line of work." He nodded at Irish. "This the new man in your life? I heard you ditched Randy. Can't say as I blame you."

Tessa's brow dipped and she stepped closer to Irish. "As a matter of fact, yes, this is the new man in my life. And why do you think that Randy deserved to be ditched?"

Nathan's lips curled back in a smirk. "He never did know how to treat a woman right. The man had everything. The best position on the football team, the prettiest girl in the school, and a college scholarship. Everything came easy to him and he took it all for granted."

"You could have gone on to college," Tessa said. "Why didn't you?"

"Not smart enough." Nathan's lips thinned. "Randy even had that going for him. He didn't have to work very hard to get good grades. He could do anything he put his mind to. I barely passed English, and I never could memorize all those dates in history. Only thing I was good at was math." He shook his head. "Yeah, Randy squandered his life. And then he lost you. Anyway, congratulations on the new man in your life. Glad to see you back in town. Don't be a stranger." Nathan turned to leave.

He'd gone two steps when Tessa called after him. "Hey, Nathan, you were there the night of our graduation party, weren't you?"

He turned, his eyes narrowing. "Yeah, why?"

"I just don't remember everyone who was there." She smiled. "I was just wondering."

"You probably don't remember because you were busy with Randy." He nodded. "I was there. I didn't stay long, though."

"Why not?" Tessa asked.

"Nothing there for me. Just a bunch of kids getting drunk. Why do you ask?"

"I just think about Penny every once in a while and wonder if anyone saw anything that would help us figure out what happened to her."

Nathan tilted his head to one side. "Like what?"

"Like if she left with somebody."

Nathan shook his head. "Nope, I didn't see her leave with anybody." He raised a hand. "Look, I need to go. I'm supposed to stop by the pharmacy for Mom's meds. See you around."

By the time Nathan left, Josh had freed up at the counter.

"Come on, let's go talk to Josh," Tessa said.

"Good morning," Josh Kitterman said from behind the counter. "What can I help you with?"

Irish set the tub of putty on the counter along with a small putty knife. "I'd like to purchase these."

"Hey, Josh," Tessa said. "Good to see you."

"Hey, Tessa," Josh acknowledged and rang up the items. "I've seen you around town, I just haven't had the chance to say hello."

"I wanted to say I'm sorry about what happened to Kitty. I can't believe I only just heard about it."

His eyes clouded and his mouth formed a thin line. "We were all pretty shocked."

"I was surprised there wasn't anything in the obituaries about her death."

Josh shook his head. "The folks had been gone so long that they only put the announcement in the Kerrville newspaper where Kitty lived."

"They ever catch the guy?" Tessa asked.

Josh shook his head. "Nope."

Tessa lowered her voice and spoke softly. "Do you mind me asking what happened?"

He sighed. "She was home with her two kids. One of them was two, the other was only eight months old. Her husband had gone out of town on a conference. He'd talked to her on the phone that morning, no problem. Everything was fine. When he got home that afternoon, he walked into the house, the door was unlocked. The two-year-old was sitting on the floor in the living room, crying. The baby was in her crib crying. Kitty was gone. He searched throughout the house, couldn't find her. Looked around the yard. She wasn't there. He called 9-1-1. The police searched the neighborhoods surrounding their house. Nothing."

"Was there forced entry on her house?" Irish asked.

Josh shook his head. "No. They think she must have known who it was because she opened the door. Her husband was pretty broken up about it. Mom's been helping him out as much as she can with the kids. They found Kitty's body alongside the interstate, a couple of days later. The autopsy reported that she had been strangled. Someone had choked her to death with his hands." The more Josh spoke, the tighter his voice became. Finally, he looked away, as if to get a grip on his emotions. "It happened while I was in the military. I couldn't talk about it for a long time. I can't imagine what she went through." His voice faltered. "My poor sister."

"Did the police have any idea who it might have been?"

Josh shook his head. "None. And no one on her street saw anybody coming or going. In her subdivision, both the husband and wife have full-time jobs. Kitty was a schoolteacher. Since it was summertime, she was home with the kids."

Tessa reached across the counter and touched Josh's hand. "I really am sorry. Kitty and I were good friends. She was one of the nicest people I know. Hard to think anybody could do that to her."

Josh nodded. "And those poor kids will never know what a great mother she was. My wife and I get down there as often as we can. We bring the kids up here when we have time off. Kitty's husband just now started dating again. I really do hope he finds somebody who can love those children as much as she did."

"Me, too," Tessa said.

As Irish paid for his purchases, Josh looked across the counter at Tessa. "I heard you ran into some trouble here recently."

She half smiled. "Word gets around, doesn't it?"

Kitty's brother nodded. "Be careful. If Kitty knew who attacked her, it could be somebody she knew from high school. Somebody from Whiskey Gulch. I mean, they never did find Penny's killer and Kitty's killer is still out there somewhere."

"Do you think they could be the same person?" Tessa asked. "The person who attacked me and the person who killed Kitty, Bethany and Penny?"

His eyes narrowed. "Deputy Jones came by earlier today and talked about the possibility. I also heard that Bethany York was murdered down in San Antonio. You were all cheerleaders and seniors in high school at the same time. It's not too far-fetched an idea."

"Did Kitty ever share her thoughts about the night that Penny died?" Tessa asked.

Josh shook his head. "I'd already left home. She'd written about it in a letter. But not her feelings about what had happened, other than she was sad that Penny was gone and that it was horrible that somebody had done that while they were all out partying. I guess she felt guilty that it happened so close and no one knew."

"I think we all felt bad for Penny," Tessa confessed.

"You know, if there's anything I can do to help you find the person who's attacking you, I'll do it. I know Kitty would have wanted me to help a friend."

"Thanks, Josh," Tessa said.

As they exited the hardware store, Tessa reached out and gripped Irish's hand. He closed his fingers around hers and squeezed gently.

"I'm sorry about your friends," he said. "This can't be easy, rehashing it." He knew what it was like to lose friends. Even though they knew the risks as a Delta Force operator, losing a brother always hit hard. "Wanna stop by the sheriff's office and then we'll go by the diner?" he asked.

She nodded. "Let's do it." She held his hand all the way out to the truck. Once there, she let him open the door and help her up inside.

He liked that she felt comfortable with him. And that she felt safe holding his hand. He wanted to find the guy that was doing this to her and take him out of her life so that she could live peacefully. Even knowing that when he did, his job here would be done. He didn't want to be done with Tessa.

Chapter Twelve

Irish drove to the sheriff's department and parked out front. Before Tessa was out of her seat, he was around the side and opening her door for her. Maybe it was part of his job to take care of her, but Tessa guessed that it was in his nature to open doors for women.

When he held out his hand, she placed hers in his and he helped her out of the truck.

"You do know I'm quite capable of opening my own doors, right?" she said.

He grinned. "Oh, yeah, I know that. Suffice it to say I enjoy opening the door for you. Please don't take that small pleasure away from me."

She smiled. "Okay. I'd hate to deprive you of your chivalrous deeds. You have to keep the shine on your knightly armor."

"That's right." He winked. "The armor has to shine."

Once inside, she spotted Deputy Jones sitting at a computer, with Matt Hennessey looking over her shoulder.

The deputy glanced up. "Oh, Ms. Bolton. Glad you showed up."

Tessa's pulse fluttered. "Have you found anything?"

Deputy Jones's lips pressed together. "Not much, but everything put together will count eventually."

"So, what's new?" Irish asked.

She pointed to the computer monitor. "We were able to get electronic copies of Bethany York's autopsy."

"And what did you learn from it?" Tessa asked.

"Like Mrs. Kitterman," Deputy Jones said, "Ms. York was also strangled. But there's something else."

Tessa stepped closer.

The deputy continued. "What was strange was that her fingers and toes showed signs of frostbite."

"Frostbite?" Tessa's forehead creased.

Deputy Jones nodded. "Frostbite."

"What time of year did you say she was murdered?" Irish asked.

Matt Hennessey turned to Tessa and Irish. "July."

"How?" Tessa queried.

"All we could figure was that maybe she'd been trapped in a freezer before her killer strangled her."

"And Kitty?" Tessa asked.

"We haven't gotten Kitty Kitterman's autopsy report yet. We'll let you know as soon as we do."

"Well, that's different than Penny's death. She was strangled and shoved off a cliff. No frostbite," Irish said.

"She was dead before she landed, according to her autopsy report," Matt Hennessey said. "Bethany York wasn't dead when she got frostbite."

"And she was found north of Kerrville off the interstate?" Irish asked.

"That's right," Deputy Jones said.

"Pretty close to where Kitty Kitterman was found. And Kerrville's not that far from San Antonio," Irish said.

"True," Deputy Jones said.

"It sounds like it's the same man who killed Kitty Kitterman and Bethany York," Matt said. "And based on the fact that Penny, Kitty and Bethany were all cheerleaders on the same squad, Penny could have been killed by the same guy. And that could be the same man who is now after Tessa."

"But what does that tell us about this man?" Irish asked.

"That he likes to strangle his victims, for one," the deputy said.

Tessa raised a hand to her throat and shivered. "And he nearly got away with it with me."

"Fortunately, he did not get away with it." Irish held out his hand. Tessa took it.

"How horrible for Bethany," Tessa said. "It's bad enough to be strangled to death, but to have to freeze before you're strangled. So cold that frostbite was on her fingertips, that's awful. He could have locked her in a restaurant refrigerator or freezer. Bethany was small. He could have put her in a chest freezer."

"In a chest freezer, she would have run out of air pretty quickly," Deputy Jones said. "Which means she would have died pretty quickly in a chest freezer. It had to be big enough for her to survive long enough for him to take her back out and strangle her. Her killer had access to a large refrigerator or freezer."

"Maybe he works in a restaurant?" Tessa suggested.

"Or a meat packing plant," Matt added.

"Is that all you have?" Tessa asked.

Deputy Jones nodded. "Told you it wasn't much, but every little clue adds up."

"We're going to find this guy, preferably before he gets to Tessa," Irish said.

"Where are you two headed now?" Matt asked.

"The diner for lunch," Irish answered.

"Is Trace holding down the fort at the ranch?" Matt grinned.

"Between his mother and Lilly, they've got everything under control."

Tessa started for the door and turned around. "Did you have any luck with your background checks on the male members of my high school class?"

Deputy Jones shook her head. "Nothing much. A few speeding tickets is all I've found so far. One DUI, but no felonies, domestic abuse or violent crimes." The deputy's gaze met Tessa's. "I understand that you left your husband because he was abusive. I didn't find anything in his background check about it." She raised her eyebrows. "You said he beat you?"

Tessa winced. "I didn't report it to the police or press charges. I just wanted out."

The deputy shook her head. "You know without a record, he could hurt someone else and the police would have nothing to go on. Abusive men are usually repeat offenders."

"I didn't think about that. I didn't want him to have a felony record. It would have made it harder for him to get work."

"It's not too late to file a report," Deputy Jones said. "You have the hospital records."

Tessa nodded. "I'll think about it." The thought of another woman suffering at the hands of her ex-husband made Tessa's stomach roil.

Deputy Jones turned back to the monitor. "We've got a few more of the guys to run through the background check and the other autopsy report to review. Should have that done before your meeting with Randy Hudson."

"Trace and I will be there for that meeting," Matt said.

"And I'll be nearby." Deputy Jones stood. "We didn't get the metal detector from the high school. The principal said it's out of commission and has a work order on it. The company that services it was supposed to be there today to get it working, but they got tied up on another job."

Irish frowned. "I'm not sure I like the idea of Tessa's ex getting anywhere close to her without running him through that metal detector first."

Tessa touched his arm. "I'll be okay. The killer likes to strangle his victims, not shoot them."

"Don't forget he tried to ram you with a vehicle," Irish reminded her.

She nodded. "I contend that Randy isn't the killer.

We'll be in a public place, surrounded by people. The killer hasn't shown his face to anyone yet. I doubt it's Randy. But maybe he'll know something that could lead us in the right direction."

"Just be careful and don't get too close to him," the deputy said.

Tessa nodded. "I'll be on the alert for any signs of guns or knives. He'd never threatened me with either, but his feet and fists did enough damage."

Irish led Tessa out of the sheriff's office and helped her into his truck. The closer they got to the meeting between Tessa and her ex-husband, the tighter his gut clenched. He wanted to call it off.

While Irish drove to the diner, Tessa sat in her seat, her mind going over everything Deputy Jones and Matt Hennessey had said. Bethany had frostbite on her fingers. Her heart squeezed tightly in her chest. Bethany had suffered tremendously before she'd died.

The case for finding her own attacker had now become a journey for justice for her three friends. "We have to catch this guy," she said aloud.

"Yes, we do," Irish agreed.

Tessa drew in a deep breath and let it go. "What do you think about me setting myself up as bait to trap him?"

"No way in hell," Irish said.

"He's killed three women," Tessa pointed out.

"And if you set yourself up as bait, he could kill a fourth."

"Yeah, but if I set myself up as bait, it will lure him out into the open. We could capture him and keep him from doing this again."

"Would that be before or after he kills you?" Irish shot her a narrow-eyed glance. "Not an option."

"What if he gets anxious about killing another cheerleader and decides to go after someone besides me?" Tessa asked.

"We're not going to use you as bait. No discussion." Irish pulled into the parking lot of the diner, switched off the engine, and turned to face her. "This guy is playing for keeps. He won't stop until you're dead or he's dead. I prefer it to be that he's the one who dies. Not you."

Tessa smiled across at him. "Would that bother you as a strike against your record? I mean, you are trying to prove yourself to your new boss."

He leaned across the console and captured her face in the palms of his hands. "Record be damned. You don't deserve to die any more than those other three ladies deserved to die. This guy needs to be caught and stopped. Besides, I kind of like you."

She smiled at him. "You do?"

He nodded. "You're strong, you're brave, and you're beautiful where it counts." Irish laid a hand over his chest. "On the inside." He moved his hand back to her cheek.

"Are you going to kiss me?" Tessa whispered, her gaze sinking from his eyes to his lips.

"Do you want me to?" he asked.

She nodded.

"Then, yes. Against my better judgement." He leaned forward and pressed his lips to hers. It was a brief kiss in a public parking lot, but it warmed her to her very core. When he raised his head, he stared down into her eyes. "We won't use you as bait."

She nodded. "All right. Let's go in and see what Marcie has to say."

This time, when Irish came around to the other side of the truck to open her door and assist her, he gripped her around the waist and lifted her out of her seat, letting her body slide down his until her feet touched the ground. She rested her hands on his chest and looked up into his eyes.

"Losing focus yet?" she asked.

He groaned. "Yes, and that's not a good thing."

She gave him a sexy smile. "Maybe not, but that kiss sure was."

Inside the diner, Tessa waved to Marge, the waitress that she'd known since she could remember, and Barb a younger waitress. And she looked around for Marcie. "Hey, Marge, is Marcie working today?" Tessa called out.

Marge shouted toward the kitchen. "Marcie, you've got company!" She glanced back at Tessa and Irish with a smile. "Are you two here to eat or to talk?"

"Both," Irish responded.

A pretty blonde exited the kitchen carrying a tray loaded with plates. "Hey, Tessa. Who's the cutie you have with you?"

"He's my..." Tessa hesitated.

Irish filled in. "Boyfriend."

Tessa didn't argue. It was easier to tell people that Irish was her boyfriend rather than her bodyguard. Although, given the number of attacks on her lately, people would probably understand why she had a bodyguard. What they wouldn't understand was how she could afford it. And, well, that would just take too much time to explain. It was easier to say that he was her boyfriend.

"Good to see you moving on," Marcie said. "Grab a table. I'll get some menus for you."

Irish chose a booth at the far end of the diner and guided her to the seat with her back up against the wall. He had her slide over and sat beside to her. It fit the role of boyfriend-girlfriend. And it felt good to have the warmth of his leg next to hers.

He put his hand out, and she laid hers in it. It was getting to be a habit to hold his hand. And he didn't ask for anything else, just to hold her hand. Randy hardly ever held her hand, even when they were dating. It was always a very possessive arm around her waist or shoulders. But never holding her hand. Tessa liked hand-holding. Tessa liked Irish. A little too much, considering she was just a job to him. She looked up at him. Or was she?

Marcie brought the menus to their table and laid them out in front of them. "Are you guys here to eat? Or do you just want coffee? Or are you going to question me like Deputy Jones did?" She gave Tessa half a smile. "I heard about what happened to you, and Deputy Jones explained how she thinks it could be related to what happened to Penny, Kitty and Bethany. Frankly, it scares the bejesus out of me."

"Could we get some coffee to start with?" Tessa asked. "And we would like to order something to eat for lunch. And then, if you have time, we'd love to talk to you." Tessa gave the waitress a gentle smile.

"Let me get that coffee and your order started, and I'll sit down." Marcie stepped back behind the counter, grabbed a tray, placed two cups on it and the coffee carafe. She came back, set the cups on the table and poured coffee into them, and then got out her pad and pencil. "What do you guys want to eat?"

Tessa ordered a club sandwich with potato chips.

"I'll have the same," Irish said.

"I'll be right back," Marcie said, and took the order to the kitchen. On her way back she called out to Marge, "Can you cover my tables?"

"Sure, go ahead," Marge said.

Marcie returned to their table carrying a glass of tea and sat in the seat across from them. "Okay, shoot. What do you want to know? Yes, I was there the night that Penny died. No, I didn't see if she left with anyone. I did walk her to her car, and stayed long enough to see her get in it. No, I didn't stay and see her drive away. As it was, they found her car exactly where it was when I left her."

"Why did you walk her to the car?" Tessa asked.

"She wanted to leave, and she wanted me to go with her."

Tessa frowned. "Why did she want to leave? It

was our graduation celebration. We were there for the night."

"She wouldn't say, but I could tell that she'd been crying, and her hair was messed up."

Tessa frowned. "Penny's hair was never messed up."

"I know," Marcie said. "That was what was so strange. I would have gone with her, but I had already had a couple of beers, and Wayne was yelling at me to come back." Marcie stared down at her glass of tea. "You don't know how many times I wished I'd gone with her. If I had, she might still be here today."

"Or you might have died with her," Tessa pointed out.

"At least then I wouldn't have lived my life feeling guilty." Marcie heaved a sigh. "I let my friend down, and she died because of it. All for a stupid boy."

"And she didn't say why she was crying or why her hair was messed up?"

Marcie shook her head. "No, she didn't. I asked her, and she said it wasn't important. She told me to go back to Wayne and enjoy the rest of my evening, that she was going home. She never made it home. She never made it to Texas A&M where she got accepted to go to college. She never got to get married and have babies. Or become a teacher and coach gymnastics. She never got to do a lot of things because I didn't go with her that night."

Tessa reached across the table and touched Marcie's hand. "It wasn't your fault. You didn't kill her, somebody else did."

"I might as well have. Not going with her signed her death sentence."

"So, do you think somebody came on to her and that's why her hair was messed up and she wanted to leave?" Tessa asked.

"It was either that or she had a good make-out session and then got into an argument with whoever she was making out with," Marcie said. "I went over and over in my mind who that could be, but she had broken up with Connor a week before that party. And she'd said that she was really done with him, that she was going to college and didn't need that kind of commitment when she had college in front of her. Especially since he was going on to the fire academy. They wouldn't see each other for four years. She'd admitted that they'd grown apart over the last year of high school. And he was there that night with Angela Bates."

"Was she hanging out with anybody else?" Tessa asked.

"If she was, I wasn't aware of it. I was too busy sucking face with Wayne. You know we were married for a year, don't you?"

Tessa nodded. "I'd heard. I'm sorry about your breakup."

"He thinks I blamed him for Penny's death." Marcie shook her head. "I didn't blame him. I blamed myself. I couldn't get over the guilt, and I could see that it was bringing him down, too. He deserved someone better than me."

"So you ended it?" Tessa asked.

"I did." Marcie gave a half smile. "And the jerk hasn't moved on and found another woman to make his wife and raise his babies."

Tessa squeezed Marcie's hand. "Have you ever thought that maybe he hasn't gotten over you?"

"He should have. I wasn't good enough for him. Anyone who'd let a friend down like that…"

Tessa squeezed her hand. "You didn't let your friend down. You didn't kill Penny. Someone else did. You can't blame yourself."

"Yeah, well tell me that in the middle of the night when I wake up with nightmares. I see her face and then I see her lying at the bottom of that cliff."

"Do you remember seeing her at all that night other than when you walked her to her car?" Tessa asked.

Marcie bobbed her head. "I remember seeing her dancing in the firelight. She appeared happy then."

"Was there anyone else around her? Maybe dancing with her?"

Marcie stared out the window. "There were a lot of people dancing that night. And the fire cast shadows."

"Think about it," Tessa urged. "Any… Anyone big?"

"There were a couple of girls with her, and there were some guys as well. I remember because their shadows were bigger. But it was hard to tell. They were more or less just silhouettes in the darkness. Come to think of it, Eddy Knowlton might have been out dancing in that firelight. He was never really a good dancer, even in before his head injury. But there was at least one other who was equally as tall. And I can't place him right now. I can't see his face in my mind.

"But then, everybody was dancing, and if they weren't dancing, then they were in the bushes or truck beds making out. I'm sorry I can't be of more help. The night was a blur. Especially after the two beers I drank. I haven't had a beer since. I'm sorry this is happening to you, Tessa. You were always good to me. You worked with me to get the routines down right, and you always made me feel a part of the team. If I could think of anything else that I remember from that night, I'll let you know as soon as I remember it."

"Order up," the cook called from the kitchen.

Marcie pushed to her feet. "That might be your order. I'll get it."

"Marcie," Tessa called out after her.

Marcie turned.

"If you ever need someone to talk to or just want to hang out, come see me. I could use some friends." Tessa's lips quirked. "But you might want to wait until whoever's after me is caught. I don't want you to get caught in the crossfire."

She smiled. "Thanks, I appreciate that. I could use a friend, too."

Marcie brought their club sandwiches to them and, for a few short minutes, Irish and Tessa ate in silence.

"So, what do you think?" Irish finally asked.

"Sounds to me like somebody made a pass at Penny on graduation night, and she turned him down."

"And some men don't take rejection very well," Irish concluded, finishing his sandwich.

Tessa pushed her plate toward him. "Do you want the other half of mine?"

"No, but we can get it wrapped up and take it home. You might be hungry later."

"I have dinner with my ex later. I guarantee I won't be hungry."

"Maybe not while you're with him, but after you come back home, you might be hungry."

"Okay, you've convinced me." She asked Marcie to bring a to-go box for the other half of her club sandwich. Once Irish paid the bill, they left the restaurant and headed back to her home at the end of the street. Before Irish could turn off the engine, Tessa put her hand over his. "I don't feel like going in the house. How about we go out to the bluffs where this all started?"

"Are you sure?" Irish asked.

Tessa nodded. "I don't think there will be any clues out there as to who killed Penny, but I don't know, maybe some memories will come back if I just go out there. I haven't been there since that night."

"Okay, lead the way."

With Tessa's guidance, Irish drove out to the bluffs where the infamous graduation party had taken place. He parked the truck, and they got out and walked around.

"This used to be the favorite place for everybody to come make out with their boyfriend or girlfriend," Tessa said.

"And after Penny's death?" Irish asked.

"I doubt anybody comes out here anymore." Tessa walked to a spot far enough away from the edge of the cliff and pointed at the ground. "This is where the bonfire was. We stacked wood for days, and some of the parents even helped. I heard that after that night, all the graduation parties were held locked down in the gym at the high school with parents hovering over the kids." Tessa slipped her arm through the crook of Irish's elbow and leaned against him. "Thanks for bringing me here."

"I wish I could make everything better for you," he said.

"You do, just by being here," she sighed. "I guess we better get back. I've got to get ready for my date with my ex-husband."

"You don't have to go," Irish said.

Tessa nodded. "Yes, I do."

"Were you with him that entire night of the graduation party?" Irish asked.

"As far as I remember, I was," she said.

"What do you mean?" Irish looked at her.

"At some point in the night, I fell asleep on our blanket. I can't account for every minute of that night. Penny might not have left in that car. Randy could have been the one who strangled her and shoved her off the cliff. I don't know. I can't rule him out. He didn't show his violent side until things went south with his job. Verbal abuse, yes. Physical abuse didn't happen until then. But that doesn't mean he didn't have it in him. Either way, I hope we'll find out something tonight."

As they drove to the cottage, Tessa thought through all the information she'd gathered that day. From what Marcie said, Penny might have been accosted by someone. That someone could have been the person who'd ultimately murdered her. At that time of night, Randy was with Tessa, unless it was at one point that she was dancing and she'd thought Randy was hanging out with his football buddies. It was possible that he could have snuck off and made a pass at Penny.

Or it could have been one of the other guys. They still really didn't have a clue. When they reached the house, Irish went through it again and cleared it before he let her go inside.

Tessa carried the box with her sandwich in it and put it in the refrigerator. "You're welcome to eat this or anything you find in the fridge. I'm going to get ready."

She dreaded the thought of meeting her ex-husband again. He always made her feel so inferior, so small. But surely all of those therapy sessions had paid off. She squared her shoulders and went to her room with the idea that the better she looked, the better she'd feel and the more confidence she'd have when she faced Randy.

Knowing she didn't have to do it alone, made her feel even better. She liked having Irish around. He never judged her. He accepted her the way she was. It also didn't hurt knowing the sheriff's department would be in the vicinity if anything should happen.

Chapter Thirteen

While Tessa got ready for her dinner date with her ex-husband, Irish made a phone call to Trace Travis.

He answered on the first ring. "It's Travis. Whatcha got, Irish?"

"Just double-checking to make sure that you and Matt will be there tonight when we meet with Tessa's ex."

"Gearing up now," Travis said. "Matt just walked in the door. I thought I'd make it a date night with Lilly, so we'd have an excuse for coming to the diner. Matt will cover the exterior along with Deputy Jones and the sheriff."

"Good, I'll carry my handgun under my jacket," Irish said.

"We'll be ready if he tries anything with Tessa," Travis said.

"I'm glad. I don't have a good feeling about this."

"You think he'll try something?"

"Even if he's not the one who's doing this, I have a feeling that whoever is, might be watching and could make his move tonight. Or I'm just a Nervous Nelly."

Travis laughed. "You've had hunches before, and those hunches have paid off."

Irish sighed. "Well, let's hope my hunch is wrong this time." He ended the call and sat at the kitchen table. Taking his 9 mm Glock out of his holster, he set it down in front of him. In less than fifteen seconds, he had it disassembled and laid out in pieces.

He dug his cleaning kit out of his duffel bag and spent a few minutes taking care of his weapon, cleaning the bolt and the barrel, and oiling them down. He checked the magazine and made sure that it was full. Then he loaded a second magazine to take as a spare. It might be overkill because it only took one bullet to kill a man, if you were a good shot. And as far as he knew, there was only one man who was after Tessa. And if it was her ex-husband, Irish might just enjoy putting a bullet in him.

When he was satisfied, he put the weapon back together, and tucked it into the shoulder holster strapped onto his back.

Irish glanced at his shirt. It was the one he'd been wearing when they'd gone around town this morning. If Tessa's attacker was not Randy and had been watching them, he would recognize Irish in the shirt. Heck, he'd probably recognize Irish anyway, but why give him any extra clues? He left the kitchen for the living room, dug into his duffel again and came up with a sky-blue polo shirt. Stripping off his shoulder holster, he pulled his T-shirt over his head.

He was standing shirtless in the living room when

Tessa stepped out of her bedroom. and emitted a soft gasp.

She wore a sleeveless red dress that hung down to just above her knees, and she looked like a million dollars. No, she was even better than a million dollars. It wasn't just the cut of the dress that made it sexy, it was the woman wearing it. Her eyes were wide, her brows arched as her gaze swept over his bare chest.

"I'm sorry," he said. "I thought you'd be a little longer."

"No, that's okay," she said. Her face flushed a pretty pink.

He pulled the polo shirt over his head and down over his torso. Tessa's gaze followed his every move.

Quickly tucking the shirt into the waistband of his jeans, he let out a low and slow whistle. "Wow, that dress."

The pink in her cheeks deepened, and she glanced down at the dress. "Do you think it's too much?"

He chuckled. "It depends on what you are trying to accomplish."

She looked up. "What do you mean?"

"If you want your ex to regret that he'd ever lifted a hand to you in anger, that dress will do it. He'll be wishing that you were still his wife and getting down on his knees to beg to take you back."

"I don't want him back," she said. "And I don't want him down on his knees to beg me to take him back. But I guess I do want him to have a few regrets."

Irish grinned. "And he should. He let the prettiest girl in Whiskey Gulch get away."

She wrung her hands. "Maybe I should wear jeans and a T-shirt."

Irish shook his head. "No, you're wearing the right thing. Does it give you confidence?"

She nodded. "I went shopping the day after I signed the divorce papers. I guess you could say it was retail therapy. When I found this dress, it made me happy. And at that moment, I needed something to make me happy. To me, red is cheerful."

Irish smiled. "And bold."

Tessa nodded. "Bold and powerful," she said. "I wanted to feel a little bit of that power, and this dress does it for me."

"Then you're wearing the right dress," Irish said. "And you look amazing."

She glanced down at her outfit. "Yeah, but I'm wasting it on my ex."

"Maybe so, but you're not wasting it on you. Or on me." Irish gave her a wink. "Promise me that if we go out on a date, you'll wear that dress."

She smiled. "You're on."

Irish glanced down at his watch. "We have about twenty minutes to get to the diner. I got my computer out. I thought maybe we could look through the internet and see if we can find anything on the guys in your senior class. I don't know what, but I thought maybe we could poke around."

She followed him into the kitchen where he'd set up his computer. "What do you think we should be looking up? I know that Deputy Jones, Matt Hennessey, and Trace Travis have been searching for any police records on the guys that were in my class."

"Yes, they have, but I want to do some general inquiries on the internet to see if there's any information about any of those class members that might not be in arrest records. Let's look up Wayne. What was his last name?"

"Payton," Tessa said.

Irish keyed in Wayne Payton in the search bar. His name only came up in the obituary for his grandmother and for the announcement of his divorce to Marcie. Nothing particularly damning.

"Who's next?" Irish asked.

"Try Mike Bradley," Tessa said.

When he typed in Mike Bradley's name, hundreds of results displayed on the screen. "He might as well be named John Smith," Irish said. He added Whiskey Gulch to the search bar. Mike's name came up as the coach at the middle school in Whiskey Gulch, and there were several articles about him. Most were about what a great coach Mike Bradley was, and some of the charity work he had done.

Tessa smiled. "Told you he was a nice guy."

"Makes me want to meet him," Irish said.

"Stick around Whiskey Gulch long enough and you will," Tessa said.

"Next?" Irish prompted.

"How about Eddy Knowlton?"

Eddy Knowlton from Whiskey Gulch came up in several news articles about his football playing from ten years ago. One in particular detailed his injury, and how he'd had bleeding on the brain and been in the hospital for a week.

"Try Connor Daniels," Tessa said. Again, there were several news articles about his performance on the football field. And then there was also his social media page, where he displayed pictures of himself in uniform, graduating from firefighter training, and receiving a commendation from the city for rescuing a child from a burning building. He also had personal pictures with his hunting rifles and the buck he'd shot, his pickup truck with the knobby tires in the background. One image showed him holding a semiautomatic rifle.

"That's disturbing," Irish said.

Tessa laughed. "Half the guys in the county have semiautomatic rifles. This is Texas. They believe it's their right."

"I can't complain," Irish said. "I own one, too."

"Yeah, but you were trained on how to use it and how not to use it."

"Makes me wish I'd brought my other gun. But it's hard to hide an AR-15 under my jacket."

Tessa glanced down at Irish's watch and sighed. "It's about that time. We need to get going."

He nodded, pushed to his feet and helped her out of her chair. "Are you sure you want to do this? You can back out right now if you want to."

She shook her head and smoothed her hands over the red dress. "No, I need to do this. If for nothing else, it helps me face my own demons. I haven't seen him since the divorce was finalized. I used to be afraid of him. I want to prove to myself that he doesn't hold any power over me anymore. I want to know that I'm finally free of him."

Irish nodded. "If at any point you feel threatened, all you have to do is say the word and I'll get you out of there."

She smiled and touched his arm. "Thank you. I appreciate that, but I want face him on my own. I want to be the one to walk away." She gave a crooked smile. "But it is nice to know that you'll be there if I need you."

They left the kitchen and passed through the living room.

"Do you want me to drive you there and drop you off?" Irish asked.

Tessa shook her head. "No. It's better if I go in my own car. I want Randy to think that I am on my own, and I don't have anybody with me."

Irish grabbed a baseball cap out of his duffel bag and slipped it over his head. "If I'm going undercover, I have to have a cover to go under." He winked.

She smiled. "You look good in a baseball cap. Makes you look like you don't have a care in the world."

"Good. Then my cover is working," he said. "And I want my looks to be deceiving." He touched her arm. "Because I have a lot of cares in the world, and they're all tied up in you."

Her cheeks flushed a pretty shade of pink. "Thank you."

She grabbed her keys and her purse and started for the door. He got there before her and held it open. Once out on the porch, he waited for her to turn the key in the lock, and he tested the knob to make sure the door was secure.

"You lead the way. I'll follow." He opened her car door for her and waited for her to get in, then closed the door.

He wanted to be with her every step of the way, but she had to do this in her own way.

Irish climbed into his truck and fell in behind Tessa as she drove out of the driveway and onto the street. He followed her the few blocks to the diner and waited for her to park before he pulled into the parking lot a few seconds later. As she got out in her red dress, he shook his head. Her ex did not deserve to see her in that red dress. He wished it was him that she was going to meet for a date. He'd show her how a man should treat a woman.

Tessa had arrived at the restaurant five minutes early for the scheduled meeting. As soon as she crossed over the threshold, Irish got out of his truck and went into the diner.

Fortunately, Tessa had chosen to sit at a booth next to another empty one. Her ex had yet to show. Irish walked past her and sat facing her from the booth behind hers. He winked and pulled his cap down low on his forehead, letting the overhead lights cast shadows, hiding his eyes and half of his face. He wished he could be in a position where he could see the expressions on both Tessa's and Randy's faces, so he could judge what was going on. But at the very least he could see Tessa's. If she showed any signs of distress, he'd be on it right away.

Irish glanced out the window just as Trace Travis's truck pulled up to the diner. Across the street in the parking lot of a real estate agency sat a sheriff's department SUV with, he would guess, Deputy Jones behind the wheel. In the far corner of the parking lot next to the diner, Matt Hennessey pulled his motorcycle into a parking space, got off, and pretended to check the mechanical functionality of the cycle's engine. The gang was all there. Now they just had to wait for Tessa's ex.

At that moment, a slick, black BMW sports car pulled into one of the parking spaces in front of the diner. A man wearing gray trousers and a white polo shirt climbed out, checked his reflection in the side mirror and then headed for the door. Based on the image in the yearbook, this had to be Randy Hudson, former quarterback and homecoming king. And Tessa's ex-husband. He had the swagger of a man who knew he looked good and took advantage of that knowledge. He smiled and waved at someone in the parking lot. And then he entered the diner.

Irish grit his teeth, his hands tightening into fists. He wanted so badly to wipe the smile off of Randy's face. The man was an animal for having beaten his wife. He didn't deserve to be in the same building as Tessa. He didn't deserve to be breathing the same air. Irish almost regretted promising Tessa that he wouldn't punch the guy.

The man stood in the doorway for a few seconds. He waved and smiled at Marge. "Hey, Marge."

Marge nodded and continued doing what she was doing.

When Randy spotted Tessa, he headed her way, smiling. Irish almost hoped that Randy would try something stupid, just so he would have the opportunity to plant his fist in the man's face.

"Tessa, sweetheart," he said and held out his hands.

Tessa kept hers in her lap and didn't stand to greet him.

"What? No hug for old times' sake?" He slid into the seat across from her, his back to Irish.

"I guess I had that coming," he said. "But I would have thought by now you would have forgiven and forgotten."

Tessa glared across the table at him.

Irish wanted so badly to go to Tessa, to pull her into his arms and just hold her.

But this was her battle. She wanted to fight it on her own.

Irish would have to sit patiently and watch as the scene played out.

TESSA CLENCHED HER hands in her lap, gritting her teeth so hard, she could feel her jaw twitch. Randy was every bit as handsome as he'd always been. In the distant past, his good looks had made her heart flutter. Now, she felt nothing but disdain for the man.

And the sooner they got this meeting over with, the better.

She tipped her head, acknowledging his presence. "Randy."

"To tell the truth, I didn't think you'd come," Randy said. "What with the restraining order and all."

She didn't respond, waiting for her ex to get to the point of the meeting.

"You look really nice," he said. "Is that a new dress?"

She bit her tongue, wanting to tell him to shut up. He had no right to comment on her dress. She wasn't his wife anymore.

His brow puckered a little when she didn't respond. But that didn't stop him. "You must be doing all right if you can afford to buy fancy new clothes."

"I make my own money," she said, "and I spend it the way I like. Not on your fancy cars, or your expensive golf clubs."

His brow creased. "Hey, I bought those with my money."

"And I paid the mortgage on the house and bought the groceries."

Randy huffed out a breath. "I didn't come here to start an argument."

"Why did you come here?" Tessa asked.

"Is it wrong of me to want to see how my wife is doing without me?"

"Ex-wife," Tessa clarified.

Randy nodded, his smile tightening. "Is it wrong

for a man to want to see how his high school sweetheart is doing?"

"Yes, if the divorce has been final for six months and she has a restraining order on him."

He raised his hands. "Hey, you didn't have to come."

She bobbed her head once. "You're right, I didn't."

"Then why did you?" Randy asked. "Could it be that you still have feelings for me?"

Tessa snorted. "Actually, Randy, I do have feelings for you."

He grinned. "Then aren't you glad you came?"

"I have feelings of regret," she said.

His grin broadened. "Think you made a mistake divorcing me?"

Tessa held back a laugh. "I regret that I wasted so many years of my life on you."

Randy's smile dropped and his eyebrows descended. "I would have though by now you'd be over being mad at me," he said. "So, I got carried away a little bit. I'd had a really bad day at work. I was laid off, if you recall."

"So, you came home and made sure that your wife had an even worse day, by beating her until she ended up in the hospital, with three broken ribs, a concussion, a black eye, and bruises over most of her body. *My* body. A girl doesn't get over something like that. It was the final game changer in our relationship," Tessa said.

"Fine," he said, "I got a little carried away."

"A little?" Tessa raised her eyebrows.

He shifted in his chair. "I was hoping you'd moved on by now. I came to tell you some news."

"I can't imagine you having anything to say that I would give a damn about," Tessa said.

"I got a new job," he said.

"Good for you." Tessa moved to get up.

Randy reached across the table and caught her arm. "I wasn't finished."

She jerked her arm away. "Well, I am," she said. Out of the corner of her eye, she saw Irish pushing to his feet. She gave a slight shake of her head, indicating that she didn't need him to step in yet.

He sank back into his seat, his lips pressed firmly together, his jaw tight, twitching.

Tessa raised her chin and met Randy's gaze directly. "Did I tell you I took self-defense classes."

"No, you didn't," he said. "Why?"

Her lips slid upward. "So that bastards like you can't use me as a punching bag ever again."

Randy sat back in his seat. "I can see this meeting with you was a mistake."

"You think?" Tessa said, still standing.

He rolled his eyes. "Geez, Tessa. I came to tell you that I'm getting married."

"Seriously?" Tessa blinked and sank into her seat. "Does she know how you treat your women?"

"No, and that's what I wanted to talk to you about. What happened between me and you—that was just a one-time thing. I saw a therapist and she helped me work through it."

"Why do you think I care if you get married?"

Tessa's eyes widened. "You don't want me to tell her. You want me to keep it a secret that you beat me until I ended up in the hospital."

"There's no reason for you and her to ever meet. So, I'm not worried about it," he said, though he didn't sound convinced.

"Apparently you were worried enough to come talk to me and tell me not to say anything to her. She needs to know what you're capable of. She needs to take that self-defense class I took."

Randy looked right and left. "Could you keep it down please?"

"Why?" she said. "So your hometown doesn't realize that their former football star and homecoming king isn't as perfect as they thought he was? Are you afraid they'll learn that you're a wife beater? Because that's what you are."

Randy's frown deepened. "I told you that was a one-time event."

"Only one time that you put me in the hospital. The rest of the times, you just gave me black eyes or bruises. It happened more than once Randy. I'm not lying to anybody about that. And your fiancée has the right to know. I can't believe you want me to lie."

Randy leaned across the table. "I'm not asking you to lie. I'm just asking you not to say anything."

"Well, forget it, Randy. I'll do what's right. We're done here."

He reached across the table and grabbed her wrist. "We're done when I say we're done. If you hate me so much, why did you agree to meet with me tonight?"

"I'll tell you why I agreed," she said through her clenched teeth. "I want to know where you were the night that Penny died."

His brow wrinkled. "That was graduation night. I was with you."

"I fell asleep sometime during that night. Were you with me the entire night?"

"Of course, I was. I was asleep, too. I drank a six-pack of beer all by myself. I crashed." His frown deepened. "Why do you ask?"

"Did you ever have a beef with Kitty? Or Bethany?"

"The other cheerleaders?" He shook his head. "I had the prettiest cheerleader on the squad. Why would I have a problem with them?" His eyes narrowed. "Again, why do you ask?"

She inhaled a deep breath and let it out. "Randy Hudson, did you murder Penny?"

His eyes widened as he leaped out of his seat. "What the hell kind of question is that?"

"Did you murder Penny? And then did you murder Kitty and Bethany? And where were you the last couple of nights? Were you really in San Antonio or were you already here?"

He shook his head. "I was in San Antonio. My fiancée can vouch for me. I was with her and her parents, eating dinner. And the night before that, I was having dinner with my new boss and my fiancée. You aren't seriously accusing me of murder, are you?"

"I'm not accusing you of anything." Tessa blew

out a stream of air. "I just figured if you could be angry enough to put me in the hospital, you might have enough anger to commit murder. Because you almost killed me."

He stepped back. "I never killed anyone. And if you start spreading any lies like that, I'll sue you for slander. If you think it hurt when I put you in the hospital, I'll make it hurt even worse when I make you go bankrupt."

She stood and faced him toe-to-toe. "Randy Hudson, you don't scare me anymore. Do me a favor and don't ever contact me again."

He grabbed her arm and squeezed it hard enough to bruise her skin.

"Let go of me," she said.

"I didn't kill anyone, and I'm not going to let you ruin my chances at my new job or with my fiancée."

"Excuse me?" a deep voice said behind Randy.

Tessa almost laughed at her relief when she saw Irish standing behind her ex-husband. The former Delta Force operative's broad shoulders eclipsed Randy's by a few inches, and he was a couple of inches taller.

Randy turned. "Butt out. This conversation is between me and my wife."

Irish took a step closer until he was practically nose to nose with Randy. "I believe the little lady said something about you being her *ex*-husband. That would mean she's not your wife anymore. Let go of her."

Randy released his hold on Tessa's arm. "There, you satisfied?"

"Are you all right, miss?" Irish asked Tessa.

She fought the smile that was creeping up the sides of her lips and nodded solemnly. "Yes, sir. Thank you."

"Can I escort you to your vehicle?" Irish asked, again as if he didn't already know her.

This time she did chuckle. "That would be really nice."

"So, are you gonna tell her?" Randy demanded.

Tessa stared him straight in the eye. "You need to tell her, and if you don't…"

"And if I don't—" he crossed his arms over his chest "—what are you going to do?"

"I'm going to file charges against you for assault and battery."

"That was in the distant past."

"Not so distant," she corrected.

His expression darkened. "It'll be my word against yours."

"The hospital took pictures. The neighbors heard my screams, and they saw you leave in your car. Are you willing to risk being hit up with charges and having a felony record?"

Randy's eyes slitted. "You're a mean woman, Tessa."

She snorted. "Pot meet Kettle."

"You won't do it," Randy said.

Tessa's lips curled up in a sneer. "Try me."

"We're done here," Randy said, and stalked out of the diner.

Tessa stood where she was until Randy's fancy BMW pulled out of the parking lot and raced down the main street and, hopefully, out of town. As soon as he was out of sight, the stiffness in her spine that had been holding her rigid seemed to collapse and she leaned into Irish's strong body. "That was hard."

He slipped his arm around her waist. "You were amazing. Like a Valkyrie on the warpath. I wanted to jump up and cheer 'Go Tessa!'"

She laughed. "Thank you for stepping in when you did."

"Do you think he's the murderer?" Irish asked.

She shook her head. "No, I don't."

Trace and Lilly entered the building.

"Was that Randy leaving?" Trace asked.

Irish nodded.

"You mean we missed the action?" Lilly asked.

"All five minutes of it," Irish said.

"Five minutes?" Tessa laughed. "It felt like a lifetime."

"And what's the verdict?" Trace asked. "Is he the one?"

Irish and Tessa shook their heads in the negative.

"He seemed genuinely surprised when I asked him about Kitty, Bethany and Penny. He only came to ask that I not tell his new fiancée that he's a wife beater."

Trace cursed.

Lilly crossed her arms over her chest. "You didn't agree to that, did you?"

"No way. No woman should ever be beaten, even if she *deserves it*, as Randy would say. Thank you for being here, and could you thank Matt and Deputy Jones?" she asked. "Now, if you'll excuse me, I'm exhausted and want to go home."

"You want to leave your car here and ride with me?" Irish asked as they stepped out into the parking lot.

"Sure," Tessa said, glad she wouldn't have to drive to the cottage. "I don't have to be at the hospital tomorrow morning. We can pick it up tomorrow."

Irish helped Tessa into the passenger seat and looked to meet her gaze. "Are you all right?"

She nodded. "I'll be better when I get home."

"You were amazing."

"I did what I had to do."

He climbed into the driver's seat and drove the few blocks to her house. Once he'd parked, he asked her to stay in the truck until he checked the interior of the house to make sure it was clear.

Tessa remained in her seat, shaking. It had taken every bit of her energy and her determination to face her ex-husband. Though she was proud of herself for keeping it together while she had been there, she couldn't help falling apart just a little bit now. The good news was, she was completely over Randy. And by meeting with him, she had shut the door to that chapter of her life.

Irish emerged from her house. "All clear," he said.

She loved that he was a gentleman and that he was a gentle man. The sooner they figured out who was trying to kill her, and who had killed Penny, Bethany and Kitty… Tessa might have a chance with getting on with her life. She might even let herself fall in love. Maybe even with a man like Irish.

Chapter Fourteen

Irish unlocked the truck door and swept Tessa up into his arms.

"I can walk," she said. "My foot is feeling better."

"Humor me," he said and carried her up the steps and through the open front door. "I'm still earning my armor."

"No, you're polishing it. You've earned it already." She wrapped an arm around his neck and leaned close to kiss his cheek.

He turned his head at the last second and captured her lips in a kiss that stole his breath away.

Without breaking contact, he lowered her legs, letting her slid down his body until her feet touched the floor.

Tessa opened to him and thrust her tongue through to meet his in a long, sensuous dance that only made Irish want so much more. "We have to stop," he murmured into her mouth.

"Why?" Tessa's hands circled the back of his neck.

"Because you're making me lose focus," he said, raising his head to stare down into her blue-gray eyes. "What if your attacker is outside this house, waiting for the opportunity to catch us unawares?"

"I'm willing to take that risk," she said and drew his head down for another earth-shaking kiss. When she paused for breath, she whispered, "I want you, Joseph Monahan." Then she kissed him again and pressed her breasts against his chest.

"You've had a rough day. You're not thinking clearly," he argued, trying to remove her arms from around his neck.

"I've never be more focused in my life. I know what I want. I'm not asking for forever. I'll take whatever I can get, even if it's only for a night." She leaned up on her toes and brushed his lips lightly. "Please."

His heart thundered against his ribs and his pulse raced through his veins. "Woman, you're making this harder than it has to be."

"Now you're talking," she said with a wicked little smile. "You don't have to sleep on the couch tonight. Stay with me."

Irish groaned. "If I stay with you, I might regret it in the morning."

"If you don't stay with me tonight, you'll regret it all night. I know you want to…" She rubbed her belly against his hardened staff.

Another groan rose up his throat. "I can't… Sweet heaven," he said through gritted teeth. "I. Can't. Walk. Away."

"Then don't," she said and slid her leg up the side of his, pressing her center against his thigh.

"Heaven help me." He bent, swept her up into his arms and carried her into her bedroom.

When he set her on her feet, it became a race to see who could strip the other the fastest.

Because Tessa was wearing a dress, Irish won. He had her naked in seconds, while she had only his shirt off and was struggling with the button on his jeans.

Irish brushed her hand to the side, flicked the button loose, kicked off his boots and stepped free of his jeans and boxers.

When they were both standing naked beside the bed, he cupped her cheek and brushed her lips with his. "You can change your mind at any time. Just say the word."

Tessa shook her head. "Make love to me, Irish." She reached into the nightstand behind her and produced a box of condoms with a grin. "I even have protection."

Irish laughed. "Were you planning to seduce someone?"

She lifted her chin. "I was planning on getting on with my life someday. I wanted to be prepared."

"Cheers for being prepared," he said, taking one of the little packets from the box and tossing the rest back into the drawer. "But first, I have to know your stance on foreplay."

She frowned. "Is this where I'm supposed to say foreplay is overrated?"

Irish rested a hand on her cheek and skimmed a thumb across her very kissable lips. "No." He touched the tip of her nose with his mouth. "It's where you tell me how you like it."

She chuckled. "No one ever asked me what I like. I really don't know."

He pulled her close in a hug that crushed their naked bodies together. "Sweetheart, tonight we're going to find out."

Once again, he swung her up into his arms. This time, he laid her gently on the bed and dropped down beside her, leaning up on his elbow.

"I'll start slowly," he said, trailing a finger along the side of her cheek, across to her lips and over the curve of her chin. He traced a path down the long line of her neck and across to one of her breasts.

"Your skin is so soft. I could touch you all day," he said. "How's it going so far?"

"Good," she said, her breath catching.

He laughed. "Just good?"

Her chest rose to his touch. "Everywhere your finger goes makes me burn there," she whispered.

He rolled her nipple between his thumb and forefinger until it hardened into a tight little bead. Moving to the other breast, he played with it until it, too, tightened and Tessa's back arched off the mattress.

"You're teasing me," she said, her voice ragged and little breathy.

"That's the idea," he said. His finger drew a path from her breast, over her ribs and down to her belly button. He dipped the tip of his finger in briefly before sliding still farther south to the apex of her thighs.

She sucked in a breath and held it.

"Are you ready?" he asked.

"Yes, please," she responded.

"Not yet," he said.

When she huffed, he laughed. "That's just the beginning. I want you to want me as much as I desire you."

"You desire me?" she asked, her voice hitching as his finger dipped between her legs.

"It's kind of obvious," he said. "But I'm not going to satisfy my urges until you've been thoroughly satisfied."

"What if I can't be...satisfied?" she asked.

Irish frowned. "Stop listening to your ex's voice in your head." He leaned over her and pressed a kiss to her lips. "You're a beautiful, desirable, and incredibly passionate woman."

She bit her bottom lip. "I've been told I'm cold in bed."

"Whoever told you that was wrong." Irish slipped his finger into her hot, wet entrance with a smile. "We have proof." Then he kissed her, stroking her center at the same time.

This beautiful, sexy woman was about to find that she was passionate and capable of coming apart with the right touch.

TESSA COULD BARELY BREATHE. Her pulse hammered through her veins, heating her body with every beat of her heart.

She'd never felt this way before. Sex with Randy had been okay at first, but he'd never taken the time to make sure she was as satiated as he was. He'd only sought his own gratification. She'd faked her release on so many occasions to make Randy feel better about his sexual prowess. He hadn't really cared about her needs or desires.

Irish touched her in so many places with his strong, gentle hands, taking the time to make sure she liked what he was doing.

When he slid his finger inside her, she was surprised at how wet she already was, and it made her even hotter at her very core.

When he withdrew his finger to the very tip, she raised her hips, wanting him back inside her.

Irish kissed her lips and slid that wet finger up between her folds, touching her there. That special little nubbin of nerve-packed flesh.

Sensations like she'd never experience before shot through her. Tessa arched her back off the bed, crying out.

Irish chuckled. "Like that?"

"Yes." Tessa moaned. "Oh, yes."

He stroked her there again, making her tingle.

"How… How…do you—" she moaned "—do… that?"

"It's not me. It's your body's reaction to being touched." He kissed her again and dipped his finger back inside her channel, swirling it around and around.

Tessa lay back against mattress, taking in deep, ragged breaths. She wanted more but she didn't know how to ask him for it.

She didn't need to. He knew what to do. His lips left her mouth and traveled across her chin and down the long line of her neck to where the pulse beat erratically at the base of her throat.

Tessa closed her eyes and moaned again.

"Don't," he said. "Don't close your eyes."

She opened them and smiled.

"I want you to see what turns you on." He slid down her body, capturing one of her breasts, sucking it into his mouth, flicking the nipple with the tip of his tongue.

His mouth felt so good on her breast that she wove her hands into his hair and pressed him closer.

He took more of her into his mouth and sucked hard.

Tessa's breath caught and held until he released her and moved to the other breast, treating it with the same finesse as he had the first.

When he abandoned both, he trailed his lips across her ribs, following the path his hands had taken earlier to the tuft of hair covering her sex.

Irish settled between her legs, parted her folds and touched his tongue to that special place she'd only just discovered could make her tingle all over.

He flicked it, sending sparks of electricity shooting through her body.

When he flicked it again, she gasped and her hips rose off the mattress.

The third time he touched her there with his tongue, she shot over the edge, her body pulsing to her release, every nerve quivering.

This was what it was all about, what she'd read about but never achieved.

"Oh, Irish," she called out.

He raised his head, his tongue leaving her. "Do you want me to stop?"

"No!" she cried.

He laughed and continued to apply himself to thoroughly satisfying her in every way.

When she finally came back to the mattress and the room around her, she sighed. Still, it wasn't enough.

"I want you," she moaned. "Inside me. Now."

He didn't have to be told twice.

Irish climbed up her body, grabbed the little packet of protection, tore it open and rolled it down over his thick shaft.

He bent to capture her lips with his. He tasted like her, making Tessa's core heat again.

Then he settled his big body between her legs and pressed his sheathed staff to her entrance.

"Are you okay?" he asked.

"Yes. Oh, yes."

He chuckled and slid into her slowly, letting her channel adjust to his girth.

Impatient to have all of him as soon as possible, she gripped his buttocks and pulled him all the way into her until he could go no further.

He filled her to full, his staff hot and hard. It felt so very good and right.

When he began to move, she moved with him, rising to meet each thrust. As he increased his speed, her body tightened with the same urgency inspired by his tongue earlier.

She peaked and shot over the edge for the second time that night, the tingling starting at her center and spreading throughout her body to the very tips of her fingers and toes. She rode the wave of sensations all the way to the end. Satiated, satisfied, and overwhelmed by the enormity of the passion burning within.

Irish thrust one last time, buried himself deep inside her and throbbed his release. For a long time, he held steady. When he bent to kiss her lips, he said, "Your ex was so very wrong."

She laughed. "How so?"

"You're a very hot, passionate woman."

A smile spread across her face. "It just takes the right partner."

IRISH SLID FREE of Tessa's warmth, rolled onto his side and pulled her back against his front, spooning her body.

"Wow," she said.

He chuckled. "That's all you have to say?"

"I have no words to describe what just happened," she said. "Please tell me you'll be around long enough for us to go through that box."

He laughed out loud and then kissed the back of her neck. "I can't think of anything I'd rather do."

She tucked her hand beneath her cheek and yawned. "I'm tired, but I don't want to go to sleep," she said. "I don't want to miss a thing."

"Don't worry," he said, brushing the hair back from her face. "There's always tomorrow."

"What if we catch the killer?" she said.

"I'm not going anywhere unless you want me to go away," he said.

"I don't want you to go anywhere," she said, and tucked his arm around her waist. "I never knew making love could feel so good."

"Like you said, it's only good when you have the right partner," he said.

"And am I the right partner for you?" she asked in a soft whisper.

Irish tightened his arm around her middle. "I'd give that a one-hundred-percent yes." He nuzzled the back of her ear. "Only, we should probably give ourselves more time getting to know each other. I mean I could be just your rebound from your ex-husband."

"There is no way that what I feel can be a rebound."

"But is it love or just lust?" he asked.

"Can't it be both?" she countered.

"We've only known each other for a few days," Irish said. He didn't want to tell her that, in his heart, he already knew. She needed time to believe in herself before she believed in them.

"Maybe you're right," she said, and yawned again.

"We need time to get to know each other. It's probably too soon to know whether or not it's love. And I don't want to be your rebound."

"You wouldn't be," she said. "And I don't want to saddle you with my hang-ups. I just got out of a really bad relationship. You deserve somebody who's not so mired in self-doubt. You left the Delta Force and fighting in foreign countries to start your life. That's hard enough without taking on someone else's problems."

"And you left your ex-husband to get on with your life."

"We both could be suffering PTSD," she said.

He kissed her temple and snuggled close. "Go to sleep, Tessa."

"You'll be here in the morning?" she asked.

He lifted her hand and pressed a kiss to the back of her knuckles. "I'm not going anywhere."

Soon Tessa's breathing became steadier and grew deeper, and she slept in his arms.

Irish lay there holding her, counting every breath and loving every minute he was with her. He had never been one to believe in love at first sight. And maybe that wasn't what this was, but certainly a person could fall in love within the first couple of days of knowing someone. He knew without a doubt, Tessa was the one for him. He just needed to give her time to come to the conclusion that he was the one for her.

He'd just closed his eyes when a cell phone rang in the other room.

Tessa stirred. "Is that my cell?"

"I don't know, but I'll go check." He slid out of the bed, padded barefoot into the other room, found her phone on the counter beside her purse. It stopped ringing about the time his cell beside hers started ringing. He pushed the answer button on his as he walked with hers to the bedroom. Tessa met him at the doorway as he answered, "It's Irish."

Trace's voice came over the line. "Irish, we need you and Tessa out by the interstate, ASAP."

Tessa's phone started ringing again.

"Allison? What's going on?" Tessa was talking on her phone at the same time. He could hear her saying, "I'll be there in a few minutes."

"There's a massive pile-up on the interstate," Trace was saying. "Need all hands on deck to help. The fire department has every available man out there and it won't be enough. The hospital has called in all the nurses. They can use help out there on the scene ASAP."

"We'll be there," Irish said, and ended the call.

At the same time, Tessa ended hers. "Did you get the same call?"

He nodded. "Pile-up on the interstate?"

She nodded and ran for her bedroom. "Did they say what happened?"

"No, just to get out there as soon as possible."

Chapter Fifteen

While Irish pulled on his jeans and a T-shirt and shoved his feet into his boots, Tessa dressed in scrubs, pulling her hair back into a quick ponytail.

"Did they want you at the hospital?" Irish asked.

Tessa shook her head. "Allison said it's so bad out there, they want people on the interstate to help the emergency medical technicians who are over-whelmed. They're calling in as many first responders as they can get from surrounding counties. But I'm here, so I can get there quicker. Until the other units get to the site, I'm going to help. Then I'll head over to the hospital to receive the incoming wounded."

"We're riding together," Irish said.

She nodded as she looped her stethoscope around her neck. She rummaged through her closets, grab-bing blankets. "Get the towels out of the bathroom," she called out. "I'm not sure what we'll need, but it's better to have stuff than not."

On the way to the bathroom, Irish grabbed his holster and slipped it over his shoulders, tucking his handgun into it. Then he shrugged into his jacket and collected all the clean towels he could find.

With the supplies in their hands, they rushed out to Irish's truck and dumped the blankets and the towels in the back seat.

Tessa hopped into the passenger seat before Irish could get around to open the door for her.

He slipped behind the wheel and started the engine. As they pulled out onto the main road, Irish could hear the screams of sirens racing toward the interstate highway. He hit the accelerator, flooring it, speeding through town. He slowed as a truck pulled out in front of them with a rotating red emergency light clamped to the top.

Tessa nodded at the vehicle. "That's one of our volunteer firefighters," she said. "They're calling up everybody."

In front of that truck, an ambulance was just entering the on-ramp for the interstate, headed east toward San Antonio. Red, blue and yellow lights flashed further down the road, lighting up the sky.

They topped a rise and started down into the chaos. As they neared, they could see the destruction.

Tessa gasped. "Oh, dear Lord."

Trucks and cars were crunched between tractor-trailer rigs. Some had been thrown off the side of the road. Others had been lifted and piled like so many Matchbox cars. An eighteen-wheeler had smashed into the backs of other big trucks. Trailers had turned over, their contents spilled across the interstate.

Whiskey Gulch's fire department was already on

the scene with their two big engines and their smaller emergency truck. Sheriffs' vehicles were stopping traffic to cordon off the area. Irish drove onto the side of the road and passed cars that were already stacking up trying to get through. When he reached the sheriff's vehicle parked horizontally across the road, he stopped.

Deputy Jones carrying a heavy flashlight, waved him down. "Sir, you can't go any farther."

Tessa got out of the truck. "I'm here to help and so is he."

When Deputy Jones recognized the two, she waved them past the barricade.

"What happened?" Irish asked as he stopped beside the deputy.

She shook her head. "From what I understand, a truck was holding up traffic, driving erratically. He sideswiped a car, which caused a chain reaction with the traffic backed up behind them. And what you see in front of you is the result."

Tessa was already hurrying forward, carrying her towels and her stethoscope. She stopped at the first EMT she came to. "I'm a nurse. Where am I needed most?" she asked.

He shook his head. "Nobody's made it up to the front of the line yet. You could start there and work your way backward. The main thing is to get them out of the vehicle if the vehicle is in jeopardy of catching fire. Then triage."

She nodded then moved forward, weaving in and

out of the damaged vehicles, stepping into the median to get around some of the wreckage.

Irish followed, determined to stay with her.

Those who could, got out of their vehicles and helped those who couldn't help themselves. Some people staggered around, blood on their hands and faces.

Tessa had already made it to the fifth vehicle in line from the front.

Irish stayed right on her heels.

An eighteen-wheeler was smashed up against another, and a car had run underneath the trailer, trapping the driver and the occupants in the wreckage.

"There are children in the back seat!" Tessa yelled. She stopped at the car and tried to open the back door. "It's locked." Inside, a child cried and a baby in a car seat was screaming at the top of her lungs. Their parents, still in the front seat, had blood on their foreheads, but they were conscious.

"Unlock the doors," Tessa called out.

"I can't," the father said. "It isn't working."

The mother, her face covered in blood, sobbed, "Get my children out of here. Please get my children out."

"I need something to break the window," Tessa said.

Irish pulled his gun from the holster beneath his jacket. He slipped the magazine from the handle and told the toddler in the back seat, "Close your eyes!"

The toddler ducked his head, closing his tear-filled eyes.

Irish slammed the handle of the weapon against the window. It cracked, but it didn't break. He hit it again, and this time the window broke. And he used the barrel of the gun to clear the glass. Then he reached inside and jimmied the door handle.

"The back doors won't open from the inside. The child safety locks are set," the father said.

Irish pulled a pocketknife out of his jeans' pocket, reached in and cut the seat belt holding the toddler in. Then he grabbed the toddler underneath his arms and pulled him through the broken window, and held him out to Tessa.

She took the child, shaking her head. "No, you need to hold him," she said. "I can fit through that window better than you to get to the baby."

He nodded and cleared the rest of the glass out of the way. Tessa handed the child to him and then shimmied through the window. When she reached the baby, she released the buckle on the child's car seat and extricated the baby. She had to sit on the seat beside it to turn around and hand the baby through the window. Several people had gathered around to receive the children.

Using the butt of his gun again, Irish yelled at the father, "Close your eyes, I'm going to break your window." The father covered his eyes and head. Irish smashed the window and cleared the glass, and then, taking the pocketknife from Tessa, he sliced through the seat belt holding the man in place. "Can you move your legs?"

"I don't know," the father said. "Let me have the pocketknife."

Irish handed the man the knife.

The driver leaned over and cut the seat belt holding his wife in the passenger seat.

"Oh, thank God. Thank God," she said.

Irish helped Tessa back through the window. The woman in the passenger seat reclined her chair all the way back and scrambled over the headrest into the back seat to climb out the window Tessa had just come through.

Once Tessa and the mother were on the ground, Irish tried to open the driver's-side door to help the man get out. It was jammed shut.

The driver tried to climb out the window but stopped, wincing. "I think something is broken," he said. "I can't move my leg."

A fire fighter appeared at Irish's side, carrying a crowbar. "Let us handle this. Move on to the next one."

Tessa made sure the mother, baby and toddler were reunited and secure on the side of the road before she hurried around the overturned semi and trailer.

An ambulance had crossed the interstate's median and was parked in front of one of the first car's wreckage. The emergency medical technicians were working to extract the driver. The ambulance was from the next county over.

Tessa approached an emergency medical technician. "You guys got here quickly."

The man ran, carrying a crowbar. "We were at the truck stop on the interstate just two exits down when we got the call. Thankfully we were already fueled up. We were just pulling out. If we'd been back at the station, it would have taken us fifteen minutes longer."

She ran alongside him as he hurried toward a vehicle that had flipped over in the ditch. "How can I help?"

"I could use someone who's got a strong back to help me pry the door open on that vehicle. There's a man trapped inside. I think there's another car farther in the woods." He turned to Irish. "Sir, I could use your help. And, ma'am, if you could go get the stretcher out of the back of the ambulance and have it ready, that would be a big help. Have you ever done that before?"

She nodded. "Yes, I have."

"Good," the EMT said. "Go. The driver will help you."

While Irish ran down into the ditch with the EMT, Tessa hurried to the ambulance. A man came running toward her. "Tessa!"

She recognized him as Nathan Harris. "Nathan, what are you doing here?" she asked.

He shook his head. "I was in this wreck. I got out to see if I could help. There's something wrong with the driver in the ambulance, he needs your help right now."

Tessa ran alongside Nathan toward the ambulance.

"What happened?" she asked.

"I don't know. He was in the back of the ambulance trying to get the stretcher out when he suddenly passed out. I got him into the ambulance but I don't know what's wrong with him. You need to check him out." When they got to the ambulance, Nathan swung the door open. As Tessa looked inside, she didn't see anyone in there.

"But it's empty." Tessa started to turn but was hit from behind, lifted and shoved into the back of the ambulance. Nathan climbed inside with her and slammed the door shut. Before she could get off the floor she felt something jabbed into her arm. Tessa fought, but he was too big, and suddenly her world became fuzzy and she couldn't control her body.

"What have you done?" she said, everything turning gray and hazy.

"What I have been trying to do for the last few days."

In the back of her fuzzy brain, her mind was screaming *No! No!* She opened her mouth. "Why?" She couldn't move. She couldn't fight. He lifted her from the floor of the ambulance and laid her on the stretcher, strapping her down.

"I got nothing but disrespect from you—from all the cheerleaders in our class. While I was out sweating on the field keeping your pretty boy from getting his face smashed in, he got all the glory. You girls only saw him. And I just got turned down by one cheerleader after the other, and slapped in the face. They never understood that ol' pretty boy Randy would never have made all the plays he made without me," Nathan sneered. "Well, he's not so pretty anymore."

"Wha…what have you…done?" Tessa said, her lips barely moving, words unable to emanate from her vocal cords.

"Your pretty boy is smashed up against a tree. His fancy car is worthless now."

Tessa fought to focus on the man's words. "It was you? You…killed… Penny."

"That bitch was the one who started all of this. I wasn't good enough for her. She slapped my face. She said none of you senior cheerleaders would ever go out with me. I was too ugly. I was never gonna go anywhere." He laughed as he tightened the second strap around her hips. "I showed them. I've been places. I've been all over this damn country."

"But you killed her."

"She fought me, but I was bigger. I was stronger. Stronger than your pretty boy. She tried to scream. I couldn't let her go crying to her friends. She slapped me. They'd take her side. So, I cut off her air so she couldn't scream. When she went limp, I couldn't leave her there for someone to find. She'd tell them. So I threw her over the cliff."

"Bastard," Tessa said.

"She slapped me. All I wanted was for her to dance with me like she danced with the other guys. A single damned dance." He turned toward the door.

"Why Bethany…and… Kitty?"

He spun back to her. "They were just like you and

Penny. Too good for me. You-all didn't have the time of day for ugly Nathan Harrison."

"Didn't deserve to die..." Tessa said.

Nathan went on, caught up in his own tale. "I caught Kitty at home with her brats. She let me in like an old friend. She never treated me like anything but dirt back in school. It was too easy to take her. I threw her in the back of my trailer and drove her out of town. When I stopped, she was so cold. I told her I only wanted one dance. One lousy dance. I'd warm her up if she'd only dance with me."

His lip curled. "Just like Penny, she wanted to scream. And, like Penny, I cut off her air so she couldn't make a noise. I gave Bethany the same chance as Penny and Kitty. She refused to dance with me. She called me a freak and fought me like a wild cat." He lifted his chin and pounded his chest. "But I won in the end."

Tears spilled from the corners of Tessa's eyes. Kitty, Penny and Bethany died because Nathan felt rejected. The man was insane. And he wouldn't stop until he'd eliminated all the girls he felt had slighted him in high school.

Tessa tried to move but couldn't get her muscles to cooperate.

"It's time to go." The former football player stepped out of the ambulance.

As Nathan closed the door, Tessa tried to call out, tried to scream, but she couldn't. She was too woozy.

The sound of a door opening and closing at the front of the ambulance indicated Nathan had climbed into the driver's seat. The engine fired up and the ambulance rolled over the pavement, picking up speed, taking Tessa away from the wreck, away from Irish and anyone who could save her from the man who had attempted to kill her twice already.

This time, he would succeed.

Chapter Sixteen

Irish worked with the EMT, leaning all of his weight and strength into the crowbar, trying to force the door of the vehicle open. It had landed upside down in the ditch. A man and his small son were trapped inside. The man was unconscious, but the child was awake and sobbing quietly, suspended from his seat belt in his back seat booster chair.

"One more time," Irish said. "We almost have it."

They leaned into the crowbar once more. The metal door creaked and groaned, and finally fell open.

Irish and the EMT fell forward with the door and the crowbar.

Irish scrambled to his feet, got down on his hands and knees and reached inside the vehicle for the little boy. He carefully wedged his pocketknife between the boy's shoulder and the seat belt across his chest and sawed at the strap until it broke free and the boy dropped to the ceiling of the car.

Irish grabbed him beneath his arms, pulled him from the wrecked vehicle, and stood.

Two firefighters joined them from another unit that had just arrived. One of them took the boy from Irish's arms. "Thank you, sir. We'll take it from here." They went to work pulling the unconscious man from the wreckage.

Irish looked up, searching the darkness for Tessa. When he didn't see her, his pulse quickened. He turned to the EMT he'd been working with. "Did you see where the nurse went?"

"She was supposed to go get the stretcher from the ambulance." The EMT looked up. "Where's the ambulance?"

Irish's gut clenched.

At that moment, a motorcycle wove through the chaos and pulled to a stop beside Irish. He recognized the man riding it as Matt Hennessey.

"Do you need assistance here?" he asked.

"Yes," Irish said. "I can't find Tessa. I was helping out over there and she disappeared. From what I understand, so did the ambulance. Where was the ambulance?"

The EMT pointed toward the front of the crash site. There was a dark lump lying on the pavement at the spot where the ambulance had been minutes before.

Irish, Matt and the EMT ran toward it.

A man in an emergency medical technician uniform groaned and rolled over.

"Joe!" The EMT bent to the man. "This man is our ambulance driver." He looked at Joe. "What happened?"

Joe pressed a hand to his head. When he brought it away, there was blood on it. "I don't know. Somebody hit me. That's all I remember." He glanced around. "Where's the ambulance?"

"It left?"

"Who took it?" Joe asked.

"We assume whoever hit you," his buddy responded.

"Well, he couldn't have gone back through the wreckage," Matt said. "They must've headed east on the interstate."

Irish turned to Matt. "I need your motorcycle. I need it now."

"We don't know that Tessa's in that ambulance," Matt said.

"No, but that's why you need to stay here and keep looking for her while I go after that ambulance. I need to find her immediately. This entire disaster might all have been staged to get her away from me. If that's the case, he's succeeded."

Matt climbed off the motorcycle, removed his helmet and handed it to Irish. "I'll alert the others. We'll look here. As soon as we get a vehicle through, we'll follow."

Irish climbed on the motorcycle, hit the accelerator and sped down the interstate, his heart in his throat, his pulse pounding. His one job was to protect Tessa and he'd failed.

Tessa must've passed out for a few minutes. When she swam back up to consciousness, someone was fumbling with the straps holding her to the stretcher. She blinked her eyes open and looked up into Nathan Harris's face. As soon as the straps were loose, she tried to move her arms. They still wouldn't respond, even with the straps free. What had he given her? No amount of self-defense lessons would save her from this.

Without saying a word, he bent and threw her over his shoulder, stepped down from the ambulance and dumped her into the back of a tractor-trailer rig. He climbed into the trailer with her and scooted her away from the edge. Then he jumped back down and closed the door.

Darkness was complete and the floor was icy cold. The hum of the motor echoed off the walls of the empty trailer. Cold air blew through, chilling her skin. She didn't even have the muscles or energy to shiver. She realized she was in the back of a refrigerated trailer. No one knew where she was. Was this to be the end of her?

The trailer shifted, moving slowly. Tessa tried to open her mouth and scream, but nothing came out.

Why hadn't they come to this realization sooner? Nathan was the one behind the murders. They'd been thinking refrigerators as in a stationary building. Not a refrigerated trailer. As a truck driver, the man had the mobility to move around the country. It all made sense now. It was too bad that she was the only one who knew.

Tessa focused on her fingers and tried moving them. Her pinky finger twitched. It wasn't much, but it was better than nothing. She'd have to regain a lot more movement pretty quickly, or she'd freeze to death before she could free herself.

The trailer lurched as it was pulled forward, bumping across uneven pavement as it slowly picked up speed. It leaned to the right, as if turning, then back to the left.

Soon, the road smoothed and the leaning stopped. They were going straight. Tessa assumed it was the interstate. Good, if he'd chosen to take a back road, nobody would know where to look for them. She prayed that Irish would soon discover that she was missing and start looking for her. It would take a miracle for him to find her before she froze.

She moved the fingers on her other hand. And then she moved her hand. Her toes tingled, and she moved those. It just wasn't happening fast enough. The cold was seeping into her bones, lowering her body temperature, making her more lethargic than the drug. She couldn't even rub her body, her arms or legs, to generate any kind of warmth. Was this the way that she was going to die?

Surely, Nathan would stop the truck soon; he seemed to have taken pleasure in strangling his victims. Kitty hadn't died from hypothermia. He'd strangled her to death after she had already gotten frostbite on her fingers and toes. If Tessa could hold on long enough for him to open that trailer door again, and rustle up enough energy left to fight her way free, she might just see Irish again. And she wanted that so badly. He'd shown her what it was really like to make love, not just to have sex. He'd cared enough to please her, something Randy had never done. Was what she felt for Irish love? Or was she risking losing herself again when she'd only just begun to find the real Tessa?

Irish was worth it. He was gentle, caring, and amazing in bed. Tessa was willing to take the risk.

IRISH FLEW DOWN the interstate on the motorcycle, pushing the bike as fast as it would go. He saw nothing ahead of him. Nothing. The traffic usually traveling this interstate had all been blocked by the wreckage behind him. As fast as he was going, surely he would have caught up with the ambulance by now. It couldn't have gotten that big a head start on him.

He and the EMT hadn't taken that long to pry the door of that vehicle open. The ambulance couldn't have gotten too far.

Hope faded. On a long, straight stretch of the interstate, he saw no taillights ahead of him, but he did see an exit. Had the ambulance pulled off the interstate at this point? Maybe it had taken a different route? The interstate was too obvious. It would be too easy to spot an ambulance driving along it.

On a hunch, Irish slowed and took the exit. His hunches had paid off on many occasions when he'd been on active duty. It was all he had to go on, and Tessa's life depended on him. And then he saw it. At the side of a brightly lit truck stop, sat an ambulance, the back door hanging open.

As Irish pulled into the truck stop, a couple of

eighteen-wheelers were pulling out. He drove straight to the ambulance and peered into the open door. As he suspected, it was empty. He looked around for anybody nearby who might have witnessed the people getting in or out of the ambulance.

A woman stood near the edge of the pavement, walking her two small dogs.

Irish drove the motorcycle over to her. "Excuse me, ma'am?"

She looked up. "Yes?"

"Were you here when that ambulance pulled into the truck stop?"

She glanced at the ambulance, her eyes narrowing. "Yeah, I saw it when it pulled off the road."

"Did you see where the people inside it went?"

She shook her head and bent to gather her two dogs into her arms. "No, there was a big truck parked right there. I couldn't see anybody getting in or out of the ambulance because the truck blocked my view. But after the ambulance parked, the truck drove away."

"Do you remember what the truck looked like? Could you describe it?"

She laughed. "Sure. It's that one right there." The woman pointed to an eighteen-wheeler crossing the road, headed away from the truck stop. It turned onto the on-ramp to the interstate.

"Are you sure?" Irish asked. "Are you absolutely positive that's the same truck?"

She nodded. "It's the only one I saw out here that had some kind of refrigeration unit on top of it. I remember being a little bit envious of the chill air it produces because the air conditioner in my car decided today was a good day to stop working. I thought, wouldn't it be nice if I had a refrigeration unit like that to keep my car cool for my little dogs?"

Irish didn't wait for her to finish her story. He hit the throttle, spun the back wheel of the motorcycle around, and raced after the eighteen-wheeler.

On a motorcycle, it wasn't like he could force the trucker over to the side of the road. And since the woman said that the ambulance had backed up to the rear of the truck, he assumed that whoever was driving the rig had transferred Tessa from the back of the ambulance into the trailer. That meant she was in the refrigerator unit. If he didn't stop that truck soon, it wouldn't matter. She'd die of hypothermia.

Wrecking the truck was not an option. He had to get to the driver. The only way to get to the driver would be to get inside the cab of that truck. He'd have to sneak up on it, or the driver could easily run him off the road.

As soon as Irish was out on the road and behind the rig, he switched off the headlights on the motorcycle. The truck built up speed on the on-ramp to the intestate.

Irish followed right behind the truck, sticking close to the rear of the trailer, so that the trucker wouldn't see him in his rearview mirrors. Already, the truck was moving faster as the driver merged onto the interstate.

Irish waited until the shoulder was wide enough

for him to drive up alongside the truck. Then he made his move, swerving to the right of the truck pulling up alongside the trailer. When he was close enough to the passenger door of the cab, he noticed there was a handle next to the door. If he could just get his fingers around that handle, he could pull himself up.

Matching the truck's speed of fifty-five miles per hour, Irish took a deep breath and murmured, "Sorry, Matt, I owe you a motorcycle." He stretched out his arm as far as he could, grabbed the handle, and pulled himself up onto the side of the truck, on the running board. As he clung to the side of the truck, he watched as the motorcycle spun out of control and crashed into the ditch. At that moment, he knew he never wanted to be a stuntman on a movie set.

Once he got his balance, he tried the handle to see if he could open the door. It was unlocked. He yanked it open. The man behind the steering wheel turned to face him, muttering a curse. Then he jerked the steering wheel to the right.

The door flew out of Irish's hand. He clung to the handle on the side of the truck, trying to retain his balance. When the driver swung back to the left, the door started to slam shut. Irish jammed his shoulder between the door and the truck and took the force of the door slamming against his body. But the door remained open.

The trailer fishtailed behind them, and the driver righted the rig, straightening the wheels to keep it from skidding off the highway. While the truck was still going straight, Irish pushed the door open and dove into the front seat. The driver slammed on his brakes, throwing Irish against the floorboard. He hit his head but blinked and rolled to his side, pulling his handgun out of the holster. The driver swerved the truck to the right again and back to the left. Because Irish was already jammed against the floorboard, he didn't roll far. He aimed the weapon at the driver and shouted, "Pull over!"

Turning his head toward Irish, the man snarled. "Or what? You'll shoot me?"

"Yes." At that moment, Irish realized the man was Nathan Harris, the guy they'd seen in the hardware store. The one who'd had an issue with Randy *having it all*.

"What do you think will happen if you shoot me? The truck will crash and everybody in it will die, including you and your girlfriend."

Irish's gut clenched. It made sense that Nathan was the one. The refrigerated truck was a dead giveaway. And if it was cold back there, Tessa would die of hypothermia before they came to a peaceful stop. The way he saw it, Irish only had one choice.

He pulled the trigger, purposefully hitting the back of the seat near Nathan's head.

"You get the next one," Irish said.

Nathan jerked the steering wheel to the left, cursing.

"Pull over!" Irish shouted.

Nathan jammed his foot to the accelerator, sending the truck speeding down the interstate.

Irish leveled his gun and shot the man in the chest. As soon as he pulled the trigger, he pushed himself off the floorboard and grabbed for the steering wheel.

Nathan slumped forward. Though he was unconscious, or dead, his foot was still jammed against the accelerator and his heavy body leaning against the steering wheel made it hard for Irish to move it and keep the speeding rig on the road. As he fought to keep the truck between the ditches, it careened down the interstate, going faster and faster.

Irish leaned across and shoved open the driver's door. The truck swerved to the right. Irish fought to straighten it at the same time as he tried to straighten Nathan's body to shove it toward the open door. If he could just get him out of the seat, he could get to the brake and slow the truck down.

But the man was dead and, like a deadweight, he couldn't be budged. Irish ended up sitting in Nathan's lap, shoving the man's foot off the accelerator and then pressing his own foot on the brake. It seemed to take forever and a lot of gear-shifting before the truck came to a complete stop. When it finally did, Irish threw on the parking brake, squeezed out of the driver's seat, and leaped to the ground. He raced to the back of the trailer and disengaged the big metal latches holding the doors shut.

Lying on the floor of that refrigerator unit was Tessa in her scrubs, her skin deathly pale, her eyes closed. A lead weight settled in Irish's gut. Was he too late?

He shook his head. He hadn't come this far to give up yet. If she had even a hint of life in her, he'd make sure she lived to see another day. He scooped her out of the back of the trailer and carried her to the side of the road. Her body was so cold and he couldn't tell if she was breathing.

He hugged her close, trying to get his body warmth into her. It wasn't enough. He had to warm her quickly. Even as warm as it was on a Texas evening, it wasn't enough. He carried her to the cab of the truck and lifted her up into the passenger seat. The engine was still running. He switched on the heater and climbed in next to her, rubbing her arms, holding her close. He still couldn't tell if she was breathing. So he pressed his mouth to hers, pinched her nose and blew a breath into her lungs.

Her chest rose and fell.

"Tessa, sweetheart, breathe," he said.

She didn't respond.

He forced another breath of air into her lungs. "Come on, baby, you have to live. I need to tell you something important. You need to wake up so I can do that."

Still, her chest wasn't rising.

He breathed another breath into her lungs. "I need to tell you that I love you. I need to tell you that I believe in love at first sight. It's okay. Really. I'll give you all the time you need to come to the conclusion that you love me, too. I can be patient, especially if it means spending the rest of my life with you. You wanted to get on with your life. I want to start my life. I want to start it with you."

When she didn't seem to take her own breath, he pressed his mouth to hers again, ready to blow more air into her lungs.

Her lips twitched. He leaned back. Her eyes fluttered open. He let go of the breath that he had been about to blow into her lungs and smiled down at her. "Hey, beautiful, glad you could come to the party."

Her lips curved into a smile. "You found me."

"You bet I did. I couldn't let a good thing get away."

"How did you find me?" she whispered.

He grinned, his heart lighter than it had been in days. "I followed my heart."

Her body trembled and she started shivering. "I'm ss-ssoo cc-cold."

He adjusted the heater vent to blow right on her. Lights flashed in the side mirror, alerting Irish to an oncoming vehicle. A big black pickup pulled up beside the truck.

Trace Travis and Matt Hennessey jumped down and ran to the cab of the eighteen-wheeler. Trace climbed up on the driver's side and pulled the door open. His eyes widened when he saw Nathan's dead body against the steering wheel. He shot a glance across to the passenger side and smiled. "Oh, thank God. You found her."

Tessa glanced toward Trace. That's when she saw Nathan's body slumped against the steering wheel. "He's dead?" she asked.

Irish nodded. "He's dead."

"He admitted to killing Penny, Kitty and Bethany. He also caused that big wreck. He said he ran Randy off the road."

Matt Hennessey climbed up on the passenger side and opened the door. "They found Randy's body in his BMW, smashed up against a tree," Matt said, "We're just glad to see that you survived." Matt looked around, "How'd you do it? How did you get him to stop the truck?"

Irish gave him a crooked grin. "I had to climb on board like a movie stuntman. I owe you a motorcycle."

Matt shook his head. "I can replace the motorcycle. I'm glad you got to Ms. Bolton in time. That's all that matters. And now that the case is solved, she won't have to live in fear of being attacked again."

Tessa glanced at Irish, her smile fading. "You did your job, you kept me alive. Now you don't have to be my bodyguard anymore."

He tightened his hold around her. "Let's get you to the hospital. We can talk about my next assignment after that."

With Matt's help, Irish transferred Tessa to Trace's pickup.

Matt stood outside the truck. "I'll stay here and wait for the sheriff. I'm sure they'll have questions and want to dispose of the body."

As soon as they had Tessa strapped into a seat belt, Trace drove his truck across the median and headed back toward Whiskey Gulch and the hospital there.

Once they arrived, Trace pulled up to the emergency room entrance, shifted into Park, jumped out and ran toward the door.

A nurse's aide ran out. "Need help?"

Trace nodded. "We could use a stretcher out here."

The aide ran back inside, returned with a stretcher and rolled it over to the side of the pickup.

Irish lifted Tessa out of her seat and laid her on the stretcher.

A nurse came out to help guide the stretcher into the hospital. "Tessa," she said. "You're supposed to be the one working, not being worked *on*." She smiled down at the woman lying on the stretcher.

"Thought you might not have enough to do," Tessa said.

"Sweetie, it's been utter chaos." She glanced up at Irish as they entered the hospital.

"We'll take her from here."

"I'm going with her," Irish insisted.

She smiled. "You must be Irish. I'm Allison. Tessa and I work together. She's told me so much about you. Tessa, do you want him to go back with you?"

Tessa held up her hand.

Irish took it and raised it to his lips.

"Yes," Tessa said. "I need him to breathe."

Allison chuckled. "Okay, then, come on in."

She wheeled Tessa to one of the examination rooms where a doctor checked her over, drew blood to be analyzed and, after receiving the test results, pronounced her all fit to go home to bed. "The drug he gave you will work its way out of your system in twenty-four hours. There should be no lingering effects. Get some rest."

"Could I stay and help the staff?" Tessa asked.

The doctor shook his head. "You need rest and plenty of fluids to flush your system. We'll handle things here without you."

Tessa nodded. "Yes, sir."

"Do you have someone who can stay with you for the night?" he asked.

"Yes, she does," Irish answered.

The doctor glanced from Irish to Tessa for confirmation.

"Yes, I do," she confirmed.

Trace met Tessa and Irish at the entrance to the ER with his truck. "Let's get you home," he said. "Once I drop you two off at Tessa's, I'll get back out to the crash site."

"I'd go with you—"

Trace shook his head. "You need to stay with Tessa. First responders from all the neighboring counties will be there to sort through the injured. As it is, I'm sure we'll just be in the way at this point. But we need to retrieve your truck, and I need to pick up Matt."

Trace drove them to Tessa's house and helped by opening the door for Irish as he carried Tessa through to the living room, laying her on the sofa.

Trace stood on the doorway for a moment. "Do you need anything before I leave?"

Tessa shook her head. "I have everything I need right here," she said, glancing up at Irish.

"She's right," Irish said, his heart filling with the look in Tessa's eyes. "We have everything we need right here."

Trace smiled. "When you're feeling better, I'll have Irish bring you out to the ranch for a barbeque. Lily and Aubrey would love to hear all about your experience." He grinned. "And so would I. We're all glad you're okay."

"Thank you," Tessa said. "I'd like to visit the ranch. I've always wanted to see it."

Trace left, closing the door behind him.

"Do you want me to carry you to your bathroom so you can shower and change into your pajamas?" Irish asked.

"Only if you'll shower with me," she said, lifting her chin.

His groin tightened, but he didn't want to read too much into her comment. "Do you need help standing? Are you still weak from the drug? Can I get you anything?"

Tessa pushed to her feet, swayed a little, straightened and then squared her shoulders. "I'm fine. I don't need help standing. I don't need you to wait on me hand and foot."

He frowned. "Sweetheart, you just went through a pretty traumatic event. I'm here. Let me help."

"I don't *want* your help," she insisted. "I no longer need a bodyguard or a babysitter."

"You don't?" His chest tightened. "Do you want me to leave you alone?"

"No," she said. "I don't want you to leave me alone. I want you to stay. But not because I need you."

"I don't understand," he said.

"I want you to stay because you *want* to stay. Not because you feel some obligation to help me."

"I *want* to stay," Irish said.

Her eyes narrowed. "Not because you think I'm too weak and too injured to be on my own?"

"Well...partly," he admitted. "But mostly because I like being with you."

"Not because I'm your assignment or your job? Not because you *have* to be with me?" she asked.

He shook his head and closed the distance between them. "I want to spend time with you." He gathered her in his arms. "I want to take that shower with you, to feel your body against mine." He pressed a kiss to her forehead. "I want to make love with you."

She melted into his arms. "When I was lying on the floor of the refrigerated trailer and couldn't move, all I could think about was getting out of there and back to you. I didn't want my life to end."

"Oh, baby. I was so scared," Irish said, crushing her to him, all the emotions he'd felt rushing back into his chest like a tidal wave. "When I couldn't find you, my world seemed to fall apart."

She wrapped her arms around his waist and pressed her cheek against his chest. "I felt cheated," she said.

"Cheated?"

Tessa nodded. "I'd finally found someone who understood me and didn't want to change me."

"You're perfect just the way you are," he said, smoothing a hand over her beautiful, silky, strawberry-blond hair.

"I'd barely had any time with you, and I wanted more." Tears slid down her cheeks, wetting the front of his shirt. "I didn't want to be cheated out of getting to know you better and using up my supply in the nightstand drawer," she said, her voice dropping to a whisper.

He tipped her chin up so that he could stare down into her watery eyes. "Tessa, I wasn't going to stop until I found you. I shouldn't have lost you to begin with."

"We're here now," she said, her eyes wide and hopeful. "Do you think we have something growing between us?"

He grinned. "I'm sure we do. At least, I know I have feelings for you. I'd tell you I love you, but I'm afraid I'll scare you off."

Tessa's eyes widened and filled with more tears. "You love me?"

"Yes," he said with a grimace. "I'm one-hundred-percent sure."

Her brow puckered and tears slipped down her cheeks. "How can you be so sure?"

"Because I couldn't imagine life without you." He cupped her cheek in his palm and brushed away a tear. "Even though we only met a few days ago, I feel like I've known you for a lifetime. You're my heart and soul. You're the woman I want to have children with, to start living my life with."

More tears trickled from her eyes. "I'm afraid."

"Damn." He could have kicked himself for rushing his declaration. "I didn't want to frighten you with my confession. The last thing I want to do is pressure you into saying you love me when you're not sure. You can have all the time you need to figure out what's in your heart. I'll wait."

She leaned up and pressed a kiss to his lips. "Thank you," she said. "Thank you for being you. It makes it so much easier to love you."

He heart skipped several beats then his pulse pounded hard through his veins. "Did you just say you love me?"

She nodded. "I was afraid to trust my feelings, after making such a huge mistake in judgment with Randy." She laughed. "And I've only just begun to like myself."

"Oh, baby, you're an amazing woman. You should be so very proud of who you are."

She nodded. "I know that now. And you helped me to realize it. I love you."

"I love you, too, but I promise not to rush you into anything else until you're absolutely ready." He hugged her close. "You love me. That's all I need to know for now."

"And you'll wait for me?"

He nodded. "As long as you need me to."

She wrapped her arms around his neck and pulled

him down to kiss her. "And about that shower?" she whispered against his lips.

"I'm all in." He swept her up into his arms and carried her to her bedroom. "Until you're ready, no strings, no commitments, just pure love."

She laughed. "I can live with that."

He set her on her feet on the floor and kissed her like there would be no tomorrow. Thankfully, they would have many more tomorrows.

They would spend them loving each other. And that life he'd promised he'd start living when he left the military started with her.

* * * * *

#2061 MURDER GONE COLD
A Colt Brothers Investigation • by B.J. Daniels

When James Colt decides to solve his late father's final murder case, he has no idea it will implicate his high school crush Lorelei Wilkins's stepmother. Now James and Lorelei must unravel a cover-up involving some of the finest citizens of Lonesome, Montana...including a killer determined to keep the truth hidden.

#2062 DECOY TRAINING
K-9s on Patrol • by Caridad Piñeiro

Former marine Shane Adler's used to perilous situations. But he's stunned to find danger in the peaceful Idaho mountains—especially swirling around his beautiful dog trainer, Piper Lambert. It's up to Shane—and his loyal K-9 in training, Decoy—to make sure a mysterious enemy won't derail her new beginning...or his.

#2063 SETUP AT WHISKEY GULCH
The Outriders Series • by Elle James

After losing her fiancé to an IED explosion, sheriff's deputy Dallas Jones planned to start over in Whiskey Gulch. But when she finds herself in the middle of a murder investigation, Dallas partners with Outrider Levi Warren. Their investigation, riddled with gangs, drugs and death threats, sparks an unexpected attraction—one they may not survive.

#2064 GRIZZLY CREEK STANDOFF
Eagle Mountain: Search for Suspects • by Cindi Myers

When police deputy Ronin Doyle happens upon stunning Courtney Baker, he can't shake the feeling that something's not right. And as the lawman's engulfed by an investigation that rocks their serene community, more and more he's convinced that Courtney's boyfriend has swept her—and her beloved daughter—into something sinister...

#2065 ACCIDENTAL WITNESS
Heartland Heroes • by Julie Anne Lindsey

While searching for her missing roommate, Jen Jordan barely survives coming face-to-face with a gunman. Panicked, the headstrong mom enlists the help of Deputy Knox Winchester, her late fiancé's best friend, who will have to race against time to protect Jen and her baby...and expose the criminals putting all their lives in jeopardy.

#2066 GASLIGHTED IN COLORADO
by Cassie Miles

Deputy John Graystone vows to help Caroline McAllister recover her fractured memories of why she's covered in blood. As mounting evidence surrounds Caroline, a stalker arrives on the scene shooting from the shadows and leaving terrifying notes. Is John protecting—and falling for—an amnesiac victim being gaslighted...or is there more to this crime than he ever imagined?

---

*Bad things have been happening to Buckhorn residents,
and Darby Fulton's sure it has something to do with
a new store called Gossip. As a newspaper publisher,
she can't ignore the story, any more than she can resist
being drawn to former cop Jasper Cole.
Their investigation pulls them both into a twisted
scheme of revenge where secrets are a deadly weapon...*

Read on for a sneak preview of
Before Buckhorn,
*part of the Buckhorn, Montana series,
by* New York Times *bestselling author B.J. Daniels.*

Saturday evening the crows came. Jasper Cole looked
up from where he'd been standing in his ranch kitchen
cleaning up his dinner dishes. He'd heard the rustle of
feathers and looked up with a start to see several dozen
crows congregated on the telephone line outside.

Just the sight of them stirred a memory of a time
dozens of crows had come to his grandparents' farmhouse
when he was five. The chill he felt at both the memory
and the arrival of the crows had nothing to do with the
cool Montana spring air coming in through the kitchen
window.

He stared at the birds, noticing that they all seemed
to be watching him. There were so many of them, their
ebony bodies silhouetted against a cloudless sky, their

shiny dark eyes glittering in the growing twilight. As this murder of crows began to caw, he listened as if this time he might decode whatever they'd come to tell him. But like last time, he couldn't make sense of it. Was it another warning, one he was going to wish that he'd heeded?

Laughing to himself, he closed the window and finished his dishes. He didn't really believe the crows were a portent of what was to come this time—any more than last time. His grandmother had, though. He remembered watching her cross herself and mumble a prayer as if the crows were an omen of something sinister on its way. As it turned out, she'd been right.

At almost forty, Jasper could scoff all he wanted, even as a bad feeling settled deep in his belly. That feeling only worsened as the crows suddenly all took flight as if their work was done.

Over the next few days, he would remember the evening the crows appeared. It was the same day Leviathan Nash arrived in Buckhorn, Montana, to open his shop in the old carriage house and strange things had begun to happen—even before people started dying.

Don't miss
Before Buckhorn by B.J. Daniels,
available February 2022 wherever
HQN books and ebooks are sold.

HQNBooks.com

Get 4 FREE REWARDS!

We'll send you 2 FREE Books plus 2 FREE Mystery Gifts.

FREE Value Over **$20**

Both the **Harlequin Intrigue®** and **Harlequin® Romantic Suspense** series feature compelling novels filled with heart-racing action-packed romance that will keep you on the edge of your seat.

YES! Please send me 2 FREE novels from the Harlequin Intrigue or Harlequin Romantic Suspense series and my 2 FREE gifts (gifts are worth about $10 retail). After receiving them, if I don't wish to receive any more books, I can return the shipping statement marked "cancel." If I don't cancel, I will receive 6 brand-new Harlequin Intrigue Larger-Print books every month and be billed just $5.99 each in the U.S. or $6.49 each in Canada, a savings of at least 14% off the cover price or 4 brand-new Harlequin Romantic Suspense books every month and be billed just $4.99 each in the U.S. or $5.74 each in Canada, a savings of at least 13% off the cover price. It's quite a bargain! Shipping and handling is just 50¢ per book in the U.S. and $1.25 per book in Canada.* I understand that accepting the 2 free books and gifts places me under no obligation to buy anything. I can always return a shipment and cancel at any time. The free books and gifts are mine to keep no matter what I decide.

Choose one: ☐ **Harlequin Intrigue**   ☐ **Harlequin Romantic Suspense**
                      Larger-Print   (240/340 HDN GNMZ)
                      (199/399 HDN GNXC)

Name (please print)

Address   Apt. #

City   State/Province   Zip/Postal Code

Email: Please check this box ☐ if you would like to receive newsletters and promotional emails from Harlequin Enterprises ULC and its affiliates. You can unsubscribe anytime.

Mail to the Harlequin Reader Service:
IN U.S.A.: P.O. Box 1341, Buffalo, NY 14240-8531
IN CANADA: P.O. Box 603, Fort Erie, Ontario L2A 5X3

Want to try 2 free books from another series! Call 1-800-873-8635 or visit www.ReaderService.com.

---

*Terms and prices subject to change without notice. Prices do not include sales taxes, which will be charged (if applicable) based on your state or country of residence. Canadian residents will be charged applicable taxes. Offer not valid in Quebec. This offer is limited to one order per household. Books received may not be as shown. Not valid for current subscribers to the Harlequin Intrigue or Harlequin Romantic Suspense series. All orders subject to approval. Credit or debit balances in a customer's account(s) may be offset by any other outstanding balance owed by or to the customer. Please allow 4 to 6 weeks for delivery. Offer available while quantities last.

Your Privacy—Your information is being collected by Harlequin Enterprises ULC, operating as Harlequin Reader Service. For a complete summary of the information we collect, how we use this information and to whom it is disclosed, please visit our privacy notice located at corporate.harlequin.com/privacy-notice. From time to time we may also exchange your personal information with reputable third parties. If you wish to opt out of this sharing of your personal information, please visit readerservice.com/consumerschoice or call 1-800-873-8635. **Notice to California Residents**—Under California law, you have specific rights to control and access your data. For more information on these rights and how to exercise them, visit corporate.harlequin.com/california-privacy.

HIHRS22

HARLEQUIN

Heartfelt or thrilling, passionate or uplifting—Harlequin is more than just happily-ever-after.

With twelve different series to choose from and new books available every month, you are sure to find stories that will move you, uplift you, inspire and delight you.

*Wounded army veteran Shane Adler is determined
to rebuild his life, along with the canine who came to
his rescue overseas. Turning Decoy into an expert
search-and-rescue dog gives them both purpose—even if
their trainer, Piper Lambert, is a distraction Shane hadn't
expected. And when he learns Piper's life is in danger, he
and Decoy will do whatever it takes to keep her safe…*

*Keep reading for a sneak peek of
Decoy Training,
the first book in K-9s on Patrol,
by* New York Times *bestselling author Caridad Piñeiro.*

He was challenging her already and they hadn't even really
started working together, but if they were going to survive
several weeks of training, honesty was going to be the best
policy.

"My husband was a marine," Piper said, but didn't make
eye contact with him. Instead, she whirled and started
walking back in the direction of the outdoor training ring.

He turned and kept pace beside her, his gaze trained on
her face. "Was?"

Challenging again. Pushing, but regardless of that, she
said, "He was killed in action in Iraq. Four years ago and
yet…"

Her throat choked up and tears welled in her eyes as she
rushed forward, almost as if she could outrun the discussion
and the pain it brought.

The gentle touch of his big, calloused hand on her forearm stopped her escape.

She glanced down at that hand and then followed his arm up to meet his gaze, so full of concern and something else. Pain?

"I'm sorry. It can't be easy," he said, the simple words filled with so much more. Pain for sure. Understanding. Compassion. Not pity, thankfully. The last nearly undid her, but she sucked in a breath, held it for the briefest second before blurting out, "We should get going. If you're going to do search and rescue with Decoy, we'll have to improve his obedience skills."

Rushing away from him, she slipped through the gaps in the split-rail fence and walked to the center of the training ring.

Shane hesitated, obviously uneasy, but then he bent to go across the fence railing and met her in the middle of the ring, Decoy at his side.

"I'm ready if you are," he said, his big body several feet away, only he still felt too close. Too big. Too masculine with that kind of posture and strength that screamed military.

She took a step back and said, "I'm ready."

She wasn't and didn't know if she ever could be with this man. He was testing her on too many levels.

Only she'd never failed a training assignment and she didn't intend to start with Shane and Decoy.

"Let's get going," she said.

Don't miss
Decoy Training *by Caridad Piñeiro,*
available April 2022 wherever
Harlequin Intrigue books and ebooks are sold.

Harlequin.com